A Recipe for Love

Adventures of an Italian Restaurateur

An Oakview Novel

By

Tanya Katnic

Annabooks, LLC.
Rancho Mirage

A Recipe for Love
Copyright © 2021, Tanya Katnic. All Rights Reserved

A Recipe for Love is a work of fiction. Names, places, and incidents either are products of the author's imagination or are used fictitiously. Any resemblance to actual events, locals, or persons, living, or dead, is entirely coincidental.

Published in the United States by **Annabooks, LLC.**
69 Bordeaux, Rancho Mirage, CA 92271
www.annabooks.com

Manufactured in the United States of America

10 9 8 7 6 5 4 3 2 1

Library of Congress Cataloging-in-Publication Data is available:

ISBN-13: 978-0-9911887-8-9

Books by Tanya Katnic

Oakview Series:

Our Mother Away from Home

A Recipe for Love

Acknowledgements

For inspiration, support, and a few borrowed phrases, I wish to thank Christopher Katnic, Roxanne Brandt, Noelle Reminiskey, Rosemary Hogan, Pamela Gibbons Toomey, Steve Viau, Annabooks, and my family.

Chapter One

One step into the Pizza Project is all it takes for a savory gift to heighten the sense of smell: the divine aroma of tomatoes, garlic, oregano and parmesan prolifically wafts through the air, as Italian cuisine is artfully crafted by manager Mario Bertolli and his crew. Garlic knots, spaghetti, and 20 kinds of pizza are some of the highlights on the bountiful menu.

The Pizza Project is a favorite among the residents of Oakview, a sleepy Southern California town known as the "City of 1,000 Oaks." Nestled among the other businesses surrounding the town square on Main Street, the restaurant is the twin to the Pizza Project #2, five blocks away. Since Mario's parents Bruno and Maria retired from managing both restaurants, he has skillfully taken over the reins of "#1,"and his brother Tommy is at the helm of "#2," if only temporarily.

This is Mario's favorite time of day—just before dawn, when lights are still glistening in the square and there is a peaceful stillness over Oakview as it quietly comes to life.

Kneading dough that will become something delicious in the hours ahead, Mario glances out the front windows—he calls them his "windows to the world"--and ponders over the impending day. Since it is late July, the temperatures will be in the low 80s at their peak, but for now it is cool and calm.

Like a sprinkling of pixie dust, Mother Nature has abundantly showered her dewy droplets over grassy areas and vehicles left in the streets.   Birdsong offers a sweet early-morning soundtrack as paperboy Mikey Walters waves mid-throw, and Mario smiles and waves back.

He loves this town and its citizens, and he loves the company of businesses that surround his own. There is Oakview National Bank, with Harley Keffer as the boss. Harley is married to Mayor Max Kaplan, who runs a family law firm located within blocks of the bank. And there is a boutique called Main Street Treasures, owned by Sabrina Patterson. Gloria Sheffield just recently opened a B & B—the Hope Inn--after becoming a widow under bizarre circumstances. Mario's best friend since high school, Steve Bridges, owns and operates Sonny's Pub, which his grandfather Sonny founded some 50 years ago.   Sandy Charles has the only bakery in town, Sandy's Dandies, and brews the best coffee in the state of California, in many residents' opinions. And Maisie Robinson has been running Oakview Cleaners next door for 30 years.

Mario is a proud member of the Chamber of Commerce, and he volunteers with the Boys and Girls Club when he has the time, often leading sports practices or games, or offering cooking lessons.

And he loves this restaurant, where every corner has been dusted with flour and where he has built a lifetime of memories. There was the magical time in seventh grade when he stole a kiss from Becky Newcomb in the break room when his father was manning the stove just on the other side of the wall. And his pre-Prom party during senior year of high school, when Bruno and Maria invited the Prom-goers slated to share Mario's limo and their parents for a celebration and a meal before heading out to the dance. After the kids were whisked off by the limo the parents stayed to enjoy their own party. And there was the painful, emotional time when his father paid a visit last year, eyes red-rimmed and tear-filled, when he revealed that his sweet Maria had breast cancer.

Thankfully, Maria's mastectomy was a success, and she and Bruno, now retirees, are enjoying an extended vacation in Sicily.

As well rounded as his life appears, Mario has never been a real winner in the romance department. He has dated off and on since his days at Oakview High School, but no special lady has caught his eye or his heart.

A good-looking guy of 30, he has jet black hair and blue eyes, a combination that has been admired by the ladies (and some men) of Oakview since he played basketball for his high school team. At six feet, he is lean and muscular, the result of his three-mile runs when he has time for them, and his often fast-paced job. One day Mario would like to settle down and have a family, but that wish remains an elusive dream.

Few people know that Mario earned a minor in English at Walker College in town, in addition to his business degree. His superpower is his way with words. Whether it is crossword puzzles or a lively game of Scrabble that he always seems to win, he loves words. It all started with the spelling bee in middle school where he won the county contest and went on to win the state title. He has always been a lover of words. He keeps that a secret from all but a chosen few.

"Hey, Mario!" The robust greeting is from Buddy Thomas, the chief cook at the Pizza Project for the past 20 years. Hired by Mario's parents, he has been a staple at the restaurant since his first day, often suggesting new menu items and sauces.

"Good morning, Buddy! How is it going today?"

"Living the dream, Boss! Living the dream!"

Buddy's ample girth shook as he laughed. He is quite a presence in his chef's hat and white uniform, which he has insisted on wearing since he took over as chief cook: short sleeves for summer, long sleeves for winter. He even has some pants altered into shorts for the hot months. For today, it is shorts and short sleeves.

A veteran of the United States Navy, Buddy landed in Oakview after his stint in San Diego aboard the aircraft carrier the USS *Theodore Roosevelt*. In the Navy he honed his cooking skills, feeding thousands on a weekly basis. A bit of an unmoored soul out of uniform, he ended up applying for a job at the Project and the rest, as they say, is history— which is Buddy's favorite subject in the whole world.

Each day he works, Buddy informs Mario about that day in history, and he slips in the requisite joke du jour. He calls the game This Day in History.

"Mario, guess what today is?"

"Gosh, Buddy, I don't know."

"July 20, the day that Neil Armstrong was the first human to step on the moon in 1969."

Here it comes, thought Mario.

"How does one astronaut on the moon tell another astronaut that he is sorry?" asked Buddy.

"How?"

"He Apollo-gises!" Buddy, cracking himself up, lets out a huge guffaw and breaks into a wide grin before getting to work.

"Pa dum pum!" He drums his palms on the counter. "I'll be here all week!"

Buddy's first task is to create tomato sauce that will be used for many of the menu items throughout the day. Utilizing a gigantic pot, he first throws in carrots, celery, onions and garlic. After the vegetables have softened, he adds crushed tomatoes, olive oil, garlic powder, salt and pepper to simmer for the next few hours. This pot will mirror one that Mario already has going on the stove.

Pesto sauce will be made next, but in a much smaller portion. It would be used for sandwiches and chicken calzones.

From giant rolls of pepperoni and salami, Buddy shaves thin slices for pizzas and sandwiches. And many vegetables, such as red bell peppers and onions, will hit the mandolin as well, for even thinner slices.

Mario has been lucky with the succession of high school- and college-aged employees he has hired over the years. He usually schedules five or six per day to take orders, assist Buddy, and bus tables, and adds two bartenders to the daily roster.

Today, Maritza Montgomery will take the first shift before her 4:00 class at Walker College, just about a mile away. She is studying English Literature and has aspirations to become a high school English teacher.

In addition to taking orders, Maritza will be in charge of crafting salads—from antipasto to Caesar to a plain dinner salad with tomatoes and red onions. Her two replacements who will be working the 4-9 shift will do the same.

The Pizza Project was a well-oiled machine for Mario, but it wasn't always that way.

A year ago, due to a huge red flag discovered by Jerry Chastain, his accountant, Mario learned that his manager at PP #2 had been embezzling for some time. PP #1 usually brings in more money, as it has a bar, but the revenue from food should have run about the same for each restaurant. Until Jerry's keen eye spotted the differences.

In the months that followed, Scott Williams had been fired, there had been a trial, and he was sentenced to six months in the California Institution for Men in Chino, California. He was slated to be released in a month.

Taking his mind off that unfortunate, painful time, Mario was brought back to the present with a knock on the door to the closed restaurant.

His friend Steve Bridges had two Sandy's Dandies coffees in hand and a huge smile on his face.

"She said yes!" Steve shouted, even before Mario could toss the flour off his hands and open the door.

"Congratulations, pal!"

The *she* in question was Mayor Max's secretary, Emi Rodgers. She and Steve had been dating for two years, and he finally popped the question. Emi would be entering the marriage as part of a package deal—her son and daughter from a previous marriage were the other part of the package. Her first husband died several years ago while on a construction site.

Mario thought of the weddings he had witnessed in the town square in the past year. First, there was the wedding of Mayor Max and Harley in October, and then the wedding of Cassie Greenwood and Pete Patterson just last month. Cassie was like a big sister to Mario. As a matter of fact, his father Bruno walked Cassie down the aisle.

One day last week, Mario happened to be looking out the front windows and spied a man proposing on bended knee in the gazebo of the town square, just across the street. What a great place for a proposal, he thought.

"Well, well, well! You have a lot to plan," teased Mario. "The bachelor party, the wedding, the honeymoon...the list goes on."

"Yeah, Emi is stoked about it all. I gave her free rein when it comes to planning, but I know that I have a lot to do on my own. Like choosing groomsmen. Would you care to be my best man?"

"Absolutely!" The lifelong friends hugged each other fiercely in shared happiness.

"Hey, congrats, Steve!" shouted Buddy from the back, having overheard the pronouncement.

"Thanks, Buddy! Okay, I have got to get to the pub and do some chopping, as I see you guys are doing. But mine entails things like oranges, lemons, and limes."

To his best man, he said, "Let's try to carve out some time this week for a drink and some planning."

"Sounds great! I will swing by the pub, have a burger and beer, and we can talk."

Mario returned to the kitchen and continued kneading dough and bantering with the main chopper, Buddy.

The front door to the Pizza Project resembled a revolving door, as usual, as Maritza walked in. She was taking a summer school course in advance of her final semester at Walker, which will be followed by a semester of student teaching.

"Hey guys! What's happening today?"

"Same old, same old," bellowed Buddy. "I am about to take my break. Anyone want anything from Sandy's?"

"I'm good," said Mario and Maritza in unison. Everyone chuckled.

Buddy went into the break room, took off his chef's hat, combed his hair and walked the block to Sandy's, a spring in his step as he anticipated the chocolate chip scones and cheerful conversation with the proprietor.

Everyone in Oakview knew that Buddy had a crush on Sandy. Break time and after-work time would often find him getting coffee and sweets and chatting up Sandy, who had never been married, just like Buddy. She was shy when it came to romance, but she was a strong businesswoman who ran her coffee shop with a deft hand and a sharp mind.

By 11:00, customers began to trickle in to the Project, and were a steady force all day. It was Thursday, so it was not as nuts as Wednesday's Mid-Week Madness, when slices of pizza were only 75 cents, or the weekend, when people seemed to come out of the woodwork. And Friday nights were hopping with Kickin' Karaoke.

Just recently, Mario made the decision to close on Mondays so that he might enjoy some free time. Twice a week, one of his siblings takes over the late shift so that he has additional "me time." Being a restaurateur is akin to being married to the restaurant. He even lives above the Project and has a ten-step commute to his small two-bedroom apartment.

Mario didn't mind crowds, but his least favorite time at the restaurant is the post-game convergence of a local sports team, when groups of about 20 noisy soccer or basketball players attack the games in the small arcade with messy fingers on the controls. The coaches seem to ignore the athletes while sipping their beer and talking about their team's chances for the playoffs this year.

Thankfully, the sports parties won't be starting for another month or so, when teams begin hosting their kick-off celebrations. A small reprieve.

On Friday Mario geared up for a long day. He would be in the restaurant by dawn and leave after karaoke, usually around 10:00, an hour after closing time. People flocked to the Pizza Project for Kickin' Karaoke, a showcase of Oakview's talented citizens.

It is a bit ironic that Steve shuts down Sonny's Pub on Fridays, which would normally be a moneymaker for any other pub. But he discovered that he was losing crowds to the Project so he chose instead to help Mario on Fridays, tending bar.

It seemed as if the entire town visited the Project en masse as 6:00PM struck.

Mayor Max and Harley were having a date night. The biological mother of their adopted one-year-old son EJ was babysitting the toddler, and her mother Beth accompanied her, just in case she needed assistance.

A junior in high school when she gave birth, Lexi Cassidy was slated to follow the baby's father to Stanford when she graduated from Bennington High School in Oakview last June. Zack Peterson had already been a Cardinal football star when Lexi was accepted to Stanford. Shortly thereafter, Zack broke up with Lexi, blindsiding her.

Lexi decided to stay home for her collegiate first year and instead now attends Walker College. And she scored a spot on the Lions' cheer squad, an activity she embraced in high school.

The Cassidys have a comfortable relationship with Mayor Max and Harley, and babysitting little EJ gives Lexi time to connect with him. She enjoys seeing him grow and witnessing the stages of his life. Right now he is tackling walking for the first time and has four teeth.

As the emcee of Kickin' Karaoke, Buddy lowers the lights and grabs the microphone. He loves his little time in the spotlight and looks forward to it every Friday.

The doors to the patio are wide open, and the patio is packed, just like the restaurant.

"Ladies and gentlemen, welcome to Kickin' Karaoke night at the Pizza Project! I am Buddy, your emcee for the evening. We have a few singers lined up already, so let's get to it. Come on up, Sandy! Let's give her a hand, everyone!"

Of course, being the gentleman that he is, Buddy grabs Sandy's hand to assist her onto the stage, even though it is just a few inches off the ground.

"Go get em, darlin'!" he whispers off-mic.

Sandy beams and begins her rendition of "Dancing Queen" by ABBA. She's not a bad singer at all, and in no time the crowd is singing along and dancing to the beat. Off to the side, Buddy gleams with delight, his twinkling eyes riveted on Sandy's.

"Great job, Sandy!" Buddy announced to the crowd as he helped her back down off the stage.

As the night wore on, more Oakview residents shared their seemingly limitless talent.

Steve stole away from the bar and joined his fiancée, Emi, for a duet of Journey's "Don't Stop Believin'," which seemed a fitting anthem to their impending nuptials. Even Mayor Max and Harley joined in the fun with Sonny and Cher's ever-popular "I Got You Babe," which got the crowd going again. More and more Oakviewites took their place at the stage.

"Okay, everyone," Buddy noted, "This lovely lady is our last singer for the evening."

As she approached the stage, Buddy asked for her name. "No names," she insisted softly out of reach of any ears or mics. Buddy merely nodded, wordlessly conveying his compliance.

In a departure from the upbeat songs that preceded hers, the striking woman took to the stage to sing "Killing Me Softly," made popular by Roberta Flack.

She was a tall blonde, with a cascade of curls gracefully flowing down to her waist. Her slight figure was enhanced by a formfitting black dress, hugging all of her luscious curves as if it were custom-made for her.

For four minutes she had the crowd riveted. Servers fell silent, mesmerized. Bartenders ceased pouring drinks. A hush fell over the room as a most beautiful voice skillfully conveyed the raw emotion of the lyrics.

Backlit by the gentle glow of the stage lights, the mystery woman appeared angelic. Her arms swayed to the soulful beat.

Mario stared in amazement at her beauty and her voice, anxious to know who she was.

As deafening applause punctuated her final note, she stepped off the stage and departed the restaurant.

With Buddy off on Saturdays, Mario had to wait until Sunday to keep grilling his friend about the person he would come to call his Karaoke Angel.

"For the tenth time, all she said was 'No names' when I asked for hers. Jeez, man, you have to get a grip! That damned broad has your panties in a twist!"

"Pipe down, you salty-tonged sailor! Okay, I just have one more question: How did she smell?"

"Like she was some delicate flower just picked and full of aromatic essence. How's that for a description?"

"Buddy, you are what I would label a juxtaposition, to use my favorite word in the English language. You have your potty mouth, but you have another, softer side of you when it comes to the ladies."

"That's me!" Buddy boasted, his two thumbs pointing back to his chest. "A very complex creature!"

At about 3:00 in the afternoon, after the lunch rush and in the lull of the day that gave everyone a much-needed rest, a silver-haired gentleman bearing a briefcase and wearing a suit entered the restaurant.

"Doc!"

"Davey!"

"Dr. Cummings!"

Everyone in the Project had a different name for the silver fox who chuckled, waved, and gave his standard greeting: "A gracious good day to all!"

Mario called him Doc, Buddy gave him the nickname Davey, and Maritza reflected his collegiate title.

No one would fault Dr. David Cummings for his demeanor, just shy of being characterized as a stuffed shirt. A college professor with a specialty in Shakespearean studies, he left his teaching career at the University of Notre Dame to relocate to Oakview after meeting his 33-year-old daughter for the first time.

David was a graduate student at Notre Dame when his girlfriend at the time, Constance Daniels, discovered that she was pregnant. They mutually decided to give up their daughter for adoption. David stayed at Notre Dame and eventually garnered a job in the English Department, and Constance moved to Chicago and began her administrative career at a high school there.

Surreptitiously, Constance kept tabs on her daughter, Cassie Greenwood, who lived a good life with her adoptive parents. Constance journeyed to California to watch Cassie play softball in high school and college, and she attended both graduations. She even subscribed to the local paper, the *Oakview Register*, in hopes of seeing any information about Cassie and to keep up with local news. She shared all of her news with David over the years.

When a principal position opened up at Bennington High School in Oakview, Constance applied for and nabbed the job.   At the time Cassie was one of the school's vice principals.

When a horrific accident a year ago eventually led to Constance's retirement, Cassie took over as principal. It was at that time that Constance revealed that she was her birth mother, and Cassie reached out to her birth father. David attended Cassie's wedding, and his future was cemented as he tearfully watched his daughter exchange vows with Pete Patterson, with Constance as the officiant.

"The usual?" Mario asked David, stepping towards the bar.

"Absolutely," replied David. "A two-olive gin martini with the slightest *kiss* of vermouth. "

"The usual?" asked Buddy.

"Yes, thank you," replied David.

The usual in terms of food didn't mean spaghetti and meatballs or a personal pepperoni pizza to David. Instead, Buddy zapped some microwave popcorn and handed it, still in its bag, to David.

A martini and popcorn. An unusual combination, but it works for the professor.

"Ah, the nectar of the gods." David sipped his drink with great satisfaction and poised to make a big announcement.

"Everyone, a toast to myself! You are looking at the new adjunct professor in the English Department at Walker College! I will be teaching two classes in the fall."

Mario, Maritza, and Buddy waved their invisible glasses and there were messages of congratulations all around.

Suddenly, Maritza had a thought.

"Dr. Cummings, what will you be teaching at Walker?"

"English 101 and Shakespearean Studies, a course utilizing the Bard's poetry and plays."

"Oh, my gosh!" she exclaimed, taking a step toward him. "I'll be in your Shakespearean Studies class!"

"Excellent, Maritza! Just excellent! We have a lot to look forward to."

With a lull in business and a blissful quiet in the Project, Mario posed a one-word question to David:

"Game?"

"Game!"

With that enthusiastic consent, Mario busted out the Scrabble board, where these two men seemed to have met their match: a wordsmith and a college professor, equally devoted to the English language and both fiercely competitive.

Since David started gracing the Project with his almost-daily mid-afternoon presence, he and Mario have had a Scrabble tournament going. The rules are simple: If business picks up or if David has to leave, the game ends and whoever is ahead is the winner. So far, it is a 5-5 tie.

"Did you get the job?"

The men had each played three words when David's daughter Cassie entered the restaurant.

"End!" yelled Mario, their signal to stop the game. "I'm ahead by one, 6-5!"

"Hello, my sweet daughter." David loved saying that name: *Daughter*. He knew of her presence all of her life, but to say the word aloud was golden to him.

The two embraced warmly, as though they had met years ago instead of only two months ago.

Cassie hadn't called him *Dad* yet; that would come in time.

"Yes! I'm the new adjunct professor at Walker College. Miss Maritza here will be attending my Shakespearean Studies class."

"That's great!" Cassie gave a thumb's up to Maritza, who was leaving for her summer school class.

Mario handed Cassie a glass of chardonnay, and she toasted her father.

"It is so great to have you here in Oakview, and I wish you nothing but the best at Walker. And, one day soon, I would love to talk Shakespeare with you one-on-one, so we don't bore anyone else! Cheers!"

Later that evening, close to closing time, Laney Prescott, the editor of the *Oakview Register*, sauntered in to the Project and sashayed up to the bar where Mario was working. She handed him a copy of the paper, dated tomorrow.

"Hey, handsome," Laney said in her honey voice, her sexiness on full display as usual, as she often seemed to be smoldering with desire. Her blouse was unbuttoned to where it was just shy of being obscene.

"Here is a page from tomorrow's paper, Mario. Thought that you might want to know that voting for the Book of Excellence begins on Monday. You might want to mention it to your customers."

"I appreciate that, Laney."

If Buddy were here, he would have fake-coughed and said "town slut" under his breath. That about sums up Oakview's consensus about Laney.

"Well, maybe we can go out and celebrate when you win, like you always do." She trained her eyes on Mario, who looked away, as if her staring could singe his eyeballs straight through.

"We'll see about that. Thank you for stopping by."

Laney pivoted and sashayed her way out the door, leaving invisible ashes in her seductive wake from her incessant smoldering.

Chapter Two

"Boys! You know the rules! No balls in the inn!"

Gloria Sheffield, owner of the recently established Hope Inn, was making blueberry muffins for the B & B, which serves breakfast daily. Also on today's bill of fare: spinach and feta cheese omelets and roasted potatoes.

A widow as a result of a freak accident when her husband carjacked the principal of Bennington High School last year, she emerged a frail, damaged person only to become a strong, savvy business owner. She was a tiny brunette with stylish short hair. The title of her inn reflected the hope that she clung to during her healing process.

She glanced at what she called the parlor, where inspirational words and phrases were stitched in throw pillows she created, reflecting Gloria's transformation as innkeeper. "Time to Shine," "Joyful Day," "Be Happy," and "Hope" were reminders to enjoy the moment and look hopefully toward the future with a renewed lease on life.

The aforementioned "boys" were her son Porter and one of her guests, Bobby Wilson. The boys were a year apart: Porter will be a senior at Bennington High School in the fall, where he is a stellar pitcher for the Boys' Varsity Baseball team, and Bobby will be a freshman at Walker College, a walk-on member of the football team.

Since Bobby and his mother Debra moved into the inn a month ago, the boys have become fast friends. The main topics of conversation were sports and girls, hardly any surprise.

It was an exciting time for Porter, as college scouts seemed to appear out of nowhere, stalking him and blending in with the crowds at games.

"Hey, I think I saw some USC recruits at your game last week," said Bobby. "They tried to hide their red and yellow shirts under black jackets. Man, the scouts are everywhere!"

"Ha!" replied Porter. "They can come and scope me out all they want. I am not making my decision until school starts. I have a few visits before I do that."

"You know what I was thinking?" asked Bobby. "It is really wild how you and I ended up at the inn together, all because of our shithead dads."

"True that," replied Porter. "True that."

When he was trying to carjack the principal, Frank Sheffield had pointed a gun to her neck. He was in a drug-fueled frenzy, having abused narcotics prescribed after an accident. He ended up dropping the gun, and it discharged, a bullet heading straight to his chest. He died minutes later.

Bobby's father, Gary Wilson, was a serial womanizer. A sales representative for a retail clothing company, So Cal Apparel, he often traveled. One day, Bobby came home sick from school and found Gary in his parents' bed with a buxom blonde. Turned out to be his secretary.

I can never delete that image from my brain, thought poor Bobby as he gaped at the lovers.

Things seemed to unravel from that moment. Bobby informed his mother about his father's cheating, Debra drained their bank account, and she and Bobby fled Chicago for the safety of Southern California. Both were thriving, happy Oakviewites.

"Okay, time to chat about the ladies." Porter gladly changed subjects. "Hey, Bobby. Have you asked Maritza Montgomery out yet?"

"No. Each time I go into the Pizza Project, I chicken out. She is three years older than I am, and as a senior, she seems as if she has it all together. I am just going to be a lowly freshman. But I love the way she looks—all tiny and compact, with her cute ponytail and tight jeans. She also sounds really sexy when she speaks Spanish."

Maritza's command of Spanish was one of the chief reasons why Mario hired her; his Spanish was spotty at best.

"How is it going with Sophia?" Bobby asked, referring to Porter's girlfriend of a year, Sophia Bennington.

"Really great. She is at ASB camp right now, and I can't wait until she returns on Friday."

Since junior year, Sophia and her twin brother Mark have been co-treasurers for their classes. They both have run unopposed, and the votes have been too close to call. The twins are grandchildren of one of Bennington's founders.

"Greetings, young men!" David Cummings was just coming downstairs for breakfast when he spotted the boys. "How goes the day?"

"Just great, Dr. Cummings," said Bobby.

He had a thought.

"Dr. Cummings, would you mind helping me choose an English class for this semester? I am torn between English 101 and Writing and Composition."

"Absolutely! Let's grab some breakfast and chat outside by the pool and get out of Mrs. Sheffield's way."

With that, they loaded up and set out to ponder the class possibilities.

Since it was Monday Mario had the day off, but his day was chock full of activities. He was interviewing Tommy's potential replacement for Pizza Project #2, as Tommy was only the interim manager and needed to return to his landscaping job full time.

He scanned the resume of Debra Wilson, who previously managed a diner in Chicago. A graduate of the School of Hospitality Business at Michigan State University, she was the head chef for the campus's Delta Gamma sorority house. She had myriad tales to tell about that gig. Some no bueno.

Debra's hobby's included pilates, hiking, and photography.

Hmm... She seemed like an interesting person—at least on paper--thought Mario.

At the sound of the Project's bell at the front door, he glanced up to find a tall blonde with her hair in a severe bun, and huge dark-rimmed glasses perched on her nose. There was no trace of makeup or other accoutrements. She clutched a clipboard, poised to take notes.

Mario stepped forward.

"Debra? I am Mario, the manager of both Pizza Project #1 and #2." He extended his hand in greeting.

"Nice to meet you, Mario," returned Debra, covering her hand over his.

"Have a seat, Debra. Tell me about your job in Chicago."

"Well, I oversaw a huge diner in the heart of the South Side for five years. During my tenure, revenues increased by 30 percent, and the restaurant had foot traffic of approximately 200 people each week."

"To what do you attribute the revenue increases?" Mario's interest was piqued.

"I was constantly listening to customers' suggestions, complaints, and concerns," said Debra. "I let those drive my decisions in menu changes, restaurant hours, and special events, such as a St. Patrick's Day party, reflecting the popularity of the city's favorite day of the year. I also hired a public relations manager, who successfully oversaw some marketing campaigns."

"May I ask why you left Chicago, in the midst of running such a thriving business?" Mario asked, wondering if his question was appropriate.

"I am sorry, but that is a personal question that I care not to answer at this time," said Debra, a pained look on her pretty face.

"Okay. Do you have any questions for me?" asked Mario, hoping to wrap up this awkward conversation.

"The job's hours are just during the daytime, correct?" asked Debra, thinking how she wanted her evenings free to be with her son.

"Yes," reassured Mario. "I will be having a night manager take over the second shift at 4:00."

Relieved, Debra thought that this could work. She felt a measure of comfort in the fact that she and Bobby were setting down fresh roots, away from her scoundrel husband and his adulterous entanglements.

"So," Mario began to sum things up, "I have a few more candidates to interview, and I will make my decision by Friday. I will be in touch."

"Thank you," said Debra. "I just wanted you to know that I give 100% to every job I have been given. I wouldn't be a disappointment."

"Thank you," returned Mario, showing her to the door.

When Debra left the restaurant, something striking occurred to Mario: She never smiled once during their brief encounter.

All day, Mario contemplated Debra's reasons for leaving Chicago and ending up across the country. Perhaps it was a chance for a new start. Perhaps she was running from someone—or something.

He had seen Bobby on several occasions in the Project, and he seemed like a normal kid who had a tremendous crush on Maritza, his cheeks deceiving him with a bright blush when he spotted her.

In time, Mario would know the answers to Debra's story.

For now, he was content to go to the Boys and Girls Club late in the afternoon, this time for a cooking class for children ages 10-13. Each class was only 30 minutes, as his students usually left the club after class to go home.

On today's menu: Italian sausage calzones with mozzarella.

Mario had donated kid-sized red aprons to the Club and brought them for every cooking class after washing them at home. They matched his adult-sized apron. He even had kid-sized rolling pins in his stash which he kept there along with other utensils.

For today's class, he had prepared some dough and the mild sausage and cheese mixture for the filling. Everything was ready to go, as his students filed in at 4:30.

It is funny how Mario never pictured himself as a teacher of sorts, but he was enjoying these occasional

Monday afternoons with a bunch of pre-teens eager for a lesson in Italian cuisine.

"Hey, Mr. Mario," said Emma Russo. "My grandmother said that the most important ingredient in cooking is love. She also uses the word k-peace all the time, like she is asking a question."

"Ha!" Mario couldn't stifle a laugh. "Emma, your grandmother is saying the word *capiche*, which is an Italian word. It means, 'Do you understand?' She is making sure that you understand all that she is teaching you about cooking."

"Oh, I get it! Thanks, Mr. Mario!" It all made sense to Emma now.

"Hello, my little chefs! I will be teaching you how to make calzones today. Those are like little hand-held pies. Let's begin as we always do by washing our hands really well."

The students scrambled to wash up. Mario loved coming here, as the facility was perfect for cooking classes. A huge, pristine kitchen afforded him the space for the usual 10-15 students.

Donning their red aprons, the class members began their lesson, which included the art of dough crimping.

When the calzones were baking, the students bussed and cleaned the tables. Mario always insisted that they leave the kitchen in better shape than when they came in.

Calzones were packed up in foil for the journey home, and aprons were left in a huge pile for Mario to clean for the next class.

As always, little Joni Kim was the last student to leave. A tiny little thing with her hair always in pigtails, she was one of the 10-year-olds in the bunch. But she seemed even younger because of her petite size, like she was a fragile China doll come to life.

Mario was especially fond of Joni, whom he took under his wing and became a sort of protector for her. And he always gave her the leftovers from his lesson—the dishes that he used as models. He found that he was bringing in more and more models each time he taught.

He worried about her food insecurities as she gratefully accepted the leftovers. And he wondered what her living situation was and vowed to himself to discover her story. Perhaps he would ask the director of the Club, Vic Chambers.

Before she bade him goodbye, Joni wrapped her arms around his leg, as she was too small to encircle his waist.

Then, she whispered, "Thank you, Mr. Mario," and left, clutching the leftovers to her chest.

Mario's heart simply melted.

Since it was early in the evening by the time he exited the Boys and Girls Club, he decided to go to Oakview Gym, something he rarely did in the chaos that was his very full life.

As he was riding one of the bicycles in the gym, Police Chief Bryan Stanley happened by.

"Hey, Mario! Fancy meeting you here!" said Bryan.

"Yeah, this is an anomaly for me," said Mario. "How are you doing?"

"Well, I was just thinking about you the other day. Did you know that Scott Williams gets out of the slammer in a month?" asked Bryan, a tentative look on his face.

"Yeah, I know. He'd better not show his face in Oakview. That's for sure."

Bryan concurred. "He'd have a lot of nerve doing that. I hope he learned his lesson the last five months in the pokey."

After Bryan left, Mario concentrated on his workout, pleased that he chose to take the time for himself. But, he had to admit: He couldn't shake the fear that crept into his mind when he thought of Scott Williams.

Still, he had four more precious weeks until Scott was free. A small cushion. A suspension of anxiety. A false sense of security.

Chapter Three

"So, do you think Davey is fruity?"

Mario whipped his head around at Buddy's question that appeared out of nowhere.

"Buddy, I know that you are fond of music—especially '70s music—and you love dancing, so why don't you take your vocabulary and boogie into the 21st century? No one says fruity these days; the word is *gay*."

"Hey, don't knock the '70s songs. They were so bitchen," said Buddy, who went to the boom box in the kitchen and tuned in to Sirius XM '70s show. "Staying Alive" electrically filled the room.

Buddy was ready to strut his stuff. He took off his chef's hat, and the middle aisle of the Project became his personal dance floor.

He perfectly mimicked John Travolta's dance moves from *Saturday Night Fever* all the way across the floor.

And, when Maisie Robinson entered the Project he picked her up and twirled around all 90 pounds of her.

"Put me down, young man!" demanded Maisie. When she was safely on the ground, she smoothed out her apron and huffed, "Well, I never!"

Buddy did an about face and boogied back to the kitchen, even doing Travolta's pointed-finger move, sky-hip, sky-hip, sky-hip. And he gleefully chuckled to himself all the way.

"Mario, I wanted you to know that I chased off a homeless man who had apparently spent the night in front of the cleaners," said Maisie, her frail hands planted on her hips.

Mario peered out of his windows to the world, wondering who might be in such a predicament.

"Maisie, I promise to talk to Chief Stanley about this. It has been a long time since we have had any homeless people camp out on the streets of Oakview."

"You do that, Mario. I don't want any trouble in or around my store."

Maisie took her little baby steps and trotted out of the restaurant.

"So, getting back to your question, Buddy," said Mario after Maisie left. "I don't think that David is gay. After all, he did father a child with Constance Daniels. I just think that his manner is refined, something that we are not used to in small-town life. He previously lived in the big city, and let's not forget the fact that he is a college professor."

"Okay, I will take your word for it," acquiesced Buddy, who was not completely convinced.

Back to work.

"Hey, Buddy," said Mario, as he was proofing dough for rising. "You missed Laney Prescott the other night. She brought in the page from yesterday's paper that announced the voting for the Book of Excellence, which has already begun."

"Boy, oh, boy! Boss, I am going to go to Dollar Bonanza on my break. I need to do some decorating to attract customers and get them to vote for us. I have an idea! Let's hang the paper off the counter, so that everyone can read about the voting."

"Great idea, Buddy! Hey, would you buy some containers for my cooking classes?" Mario passed him a five dollar bill, keeping little Joni in mind.

Buddy's favorite place in the whole world—besides Sandy's Dandies—was Dollar Bonanza, which he once alliteratively dubbed "a treasure trove of treats."

Mario grabbed the paper from the break room and positioned it so that everyone could see the ad about the voting when they placed their orders.

When he returned from his break, Buddy entered the restaurant carrying 10 colorful star balloons in red, white, and blue. It was a nod to good old American voting. In his pocket were packages of pencils inscribed with "Thank you for your kindness" messages on them.

"So, I am going to plant these balloons all around the Project, and you should give a pencil to the customers when they pay for their meals," he suggested. "Here are your containers. What a bargain! Six for a buck! I took care of the tax."

"Thanks, Buddy."

For the past two years, Oakview voted Pizza Project #1, Pizza Project #2, and Primavera as the top three in the Best Italian Restaurant category in the Book of Excellence, which highlighted all of the favorites of Oakviewites. There were many categories in the Book, including Best Small Business (non-restaurant) and Best Mechanic.

Pleased with his handiwork, Buddy proclaimed, with a fist in the air, "Let the voting begin!"

Sitting in his room at Hope Inn, Bobby Wilson devised a plan to exhibit his admiration for Maritza Montgomery: He would become her secret admirer and send her verses of poetry. He Googled "love poems" and came up with several; he lighted on William Shakespeare's "Sonnet 18."

"Shall I compare thee to a summer's day?
Thou art more lovely and more temperate."

The first two lines of the poem would do the trick. Bobby cut and pasted them and added a personal message: *With fondness from your secret admirer.*

He walked the five blocks to the Pizza Project and slipped the letter into the mailbox under the cover of darkness.

The next day, Mario, Buddy, Maritza and David were enjoying some friendly banter in the lovely lull of the afternoon. A lively game of Scrabble found David in the lead, having placed his first word of the game on the board.

"Javelin?" exclaimed Mario. "You're like a damn magician, pulling that out of a hat." After a quick count, he burst out, "That is worth 100 points! Twenty-five times two for the double first word, and 50 extra for using all 7!! You little brat!"

David laughed and, blowing on his knuckles, wiped them on his shirt.

Mario pondered his rack of letters; the only shining spot was an X.

Then something jogged his memory, taking him momentarily away from what would most likely be a win for David.

"Maritza, take a look on the counter. You have some mail."

Curious, Maritza perused the envelope and opened its contents.

"Wait! What? You guys, apparently I have a secret admirer!"

She passed the note to David, who, of course, knew the source of the verse.

"Well, Miss Maritza, your secret admirer is quoting William Shakespeare and his 'Sonnet 18.' In this sonnet, he seeks to immortalize his love in the lines of the poem. An impressive choice to show one's affection," he remarked.

Everyone started talking at once, and the inevitable questions arose: Did Maritza have any idea who it might be? Since there was no postmark, someone must have dropped it in the box. Who would that be?

Maritza was speechless. She had no clue as to the identity of her admirer.

After the collective musings, Buddy and Maritza got back to work and David and Mario continued their Scrabble challenge.

"Okay," Mario said glumly, "I've got oxen for 13 points."

They were actually halfway through the game when a party of six entered the restaurant.

"End!" declared Mario.

"End!" seconded David.

And the score was 6-6.

With his sister Sadie taking the late shift that evening, Mario finally had time to stop by Sonny's Pub for a burger and chat with his friend Steve Bridges. As always, the pub was bustling, as music emanated from the speakers and several couples took to the dance floor.

Mario sidled up to the bar, with no need to peruse the menu. Steve knew that he wanted a cheeseburger and a beer.

"Mario! Glad to finally see you! Been wondering where you've been."

"Hey, Steve! Got lots going on right now. I am interviewing for the manager position at PP #2, running #1, teaching cooking at the Boys and Girls Club, and just trying to juggle it all!"

"Changing subjects," said Steve. "What did you think of the last singer at Kickin' Karaoke? Wasn't she something?"

"I was completely fascinated by her," confessed Mario. "Buddy has been giving me grief since Friday."

"Ha! I would be fascinated, too, if I weren't so in love with Emi. What do you know about her? I haven't seen her in town before."

Mario put his beer down, his contemplative face reflecting his desire to know more about Miss Anonymous— just a few morsels, even a name.

"Well, she is a mystery to me. She wouldn't even give Buddy her name when he was about to introduce her to the crowd. He and I call her Miss Anonymous."

"Let me know if you find out anything about Miss Anonymous."

Early Friday morning, the Chamber of Commerce met in Sandy's Dandies. All of the business owners took turns hosting the monthly meetings, and it was Sandy's turn on this beautiful August morning, the sun bright and warm already.

The town square looked festive, and the gazebo was decorated with plastic shovels and flip flops, the handiwork of Emi Rodgers, Mayor Max's administrative assistant. The decorations were also round-robin arrangements.

As the current president of the Chamber, Mario addressed his friends:

"Welcome, everyone. Hope that you are all doing well. First off, I would like to thank Sandy for being a gracious hostess, as always. And thanks to our visitor, Buddy, for his awesome hosting duties."

Buddy smiled at the crowd, lifting a coffee pot as in a toast. When Chamber meetings were held at the Project or at Sandy's, he always made a guest appearance.

"Hey, Buddy, what happened on this day in history?" asked Steve. Everyone knew about Buddy's love of history.

"August 2, 1923: Calvin Coolidge becomes President upon the death of Warren G. Harding. Widely known as a witty chap of few words, he once was sitting at a dinner party with a woman who said, 'I'll bet I can get more than two words out of you.' Old Cal replied, 'You lose.'"

Buddy bowed with delight.

After the applause, Mario continued.

"First order of business is the pricing of the tidbits at Taste of Oakview, four weeks away on Saturday, August 30, as part of our So Long Summer weekend celebration.

Should we keep our present prices of 50 cents and two for a dollar? Or, do you want to raise them this year?"

Sabrina Patterson commented, "I move that we freeze the prices. I think that people would want to purchase more treats if they remain at the same prices."

"I second the motion," said Mayor Max, who yearly felt a challenge to come up with something yummy for the Taste. He always gave a little speech welcoming guests to the festivities on Friday night, which include carnival rides and a spaghetti dinner to cap off the weekend. It was an end-of-summer Oakview tradition.

"Okay, prices will remain the same," declared Mario.

He added, "Don't forget that the proceeds from the Taste tip jars will go towards programs and athletic equipment for the Boys and Girls Club. Sandy, thank you for saving up 10 coffee cans for the tips. My little chefs will be decorating them before the event."

After the group went on to discuss some unfinished business—such as new signage at Sabrina's Main Street Treasures and the addition of a new streetlight on Browning Avenue—Mario asked if there were any other agenda items.

Maisie raised her hand, waving it side to side.

"I am still upset about that homeless guy who slept on the doorstep of the cleaners."

Chief Stanley stood and turned to Maisie.

"Maisie, I want you to know that we have been assigning extra patrols on Main Street. I personally didn't see the person, but I will have my eyes and ears out for a potential repeat visit."

"Thank you, Chief." Maisie seemed to gain comfort from Bryan's promise.

Mario concluded the meeting by noting that the next meeting would be September 3.

Just as he was about to exit Sandy's Dandies, Laney came flying into the bakery. Her blouse buttons would make the fashion police collectively gasp.

"What did I miss?" she queried, breathless, landing in Mario's personal space.

Mario must have felt like a gleeful teacher whose obnoxious student is absent, only to have her arrive mid-class after a damn dental appointment.

Mario filled her in on everything, including the appearance of the homeless person.

"Oh, I don't like the sound of that," fretted Laney. "Not in our little town."

"Well, I don't either. Best we just say that time will tell on this one."

As Mario was fetching the mail mid-afternoon, he noticed another letter for Maritza. She had received two others after the initial missive, with verses from the E.E. Cummings poem "[i carry your heart with me (i carry it in]" and Christopher Marlow's "The Passionate Shepherd to His Love."

The secret admirer's choices were "poetically diverse," according to David.

Maritza wasn't working until Tuesday because she was concentrating on summer final exams, so Mario would have to find out then about the contents of the hot mail.

He was surprised that David didn't stop by for his usual martini and popcorn treat when he spotted him that evening before Kickin' Karaoke.

"Doc! Good to see you on a Friday night! I think this is a first." Mario welcomed him and asked, "The usual?"

"Yes, thanks, young Mario. I am here to support both my daughter and my son-in-law! Cassie is performing and Pete is the visiting DJ, as you know, giving Buddy the night off."

"Wow, I knew about Pete, but I didn't know about Cassie." Mario was shocked. "I have never seen her perform."

"She and her best friend Ellie are reprising the number that garnered them first place in the Bennington High School talent show," David said proudly.

"Wow! I am really looking forward to that." Mario loved Cassie, whom he called "Sis."

As usual, the Project was packed by 6:00. All of Mario's employees were on hand, minus Buddy. It seemed he had a date with Sandy, their first one. More to chat about on Sunday!

DJ PJ Panda—aka Pete Patterson—started the festivities by introducing himself.

"Hey, everyone! I am DJ PJ Panda from KFUNN 105.7! I am happy to be your guest DJ for the evening. First up is Sabrina Patterson of Main Street Treasures, singing Whitney Houston's "I Wanna Dance with Somebody.""

Sabrina just killed it, and the group started to fill the dance floor, which had been cleared of tables earlier in the evening.

It seemed as if Kickin' Karaoke brought out the hidden talent in so many Oakviewites that it came as a complete surprise to most everyone.

Next up were Cassie and Ellie, decked out in what appeared to be lettermen's jackets from Bennington football players.

"If we do this number anymore, we are going to have to buy our own jackets!" chuckled Cassie. "Thank goodness Coach Reddick so generously let us borrow these again."

Pete did the introductions: "Ladies and gentlemen, our next performers are best friends Cassie and Ellie. My wife is number 15!"

With that, he cued up the music to Salt-N-Pepa's "Push It."

The ladies were spot-on with the dance number. They mimicked the stars' penchant for large jackets. With

Cassie's long brunette hair and Ellie's short blonde curls, they did represent salt and pepper.

Pete even sang the few lines that the DJ in the official music video sang. That was a new one for him!

The crowd went nuts. There were even a few audience members who knew the dance moves. It was a wild time at the Project!

"That's my girl!" David boasted to Mario, who was tending bar.

"Way to go, Sis!" Mario shouted out.

When the number was over, Cassie kissed and thanked her husband and headed to the bar, and her father.

"Cassie, that was simply splendid!" David embraced her, holding on extra tight. "You and Ellie are quite the songstresses!"

"Thanks! The kids at Bennie went crazy when we performed that song. They had no idea that their principal and her administrative assistant could dance!"

"Let me buy you a drink," David said as he turned to order a glass of wine from Mario. "We can have a little chat while Pete works."

Pete was prepared to finish his gig when he announced the final act of the evening.

"I want to thank Mario for allowing me to guest-DJ tonight. It was so much fun! I usually spin the tunes in my small office at KFUNN, and it is so great to be around all of you. I was asked to remind you that Kickin' Karaoke ends the weekend after So Long Summer, so make sure that you get in on all of the fun in the next few weeks."

He concluded with an introduction to the last act: "This final couple will be performing to the song 'Just Give Me a Reason' by P!nk, featuring Nate Ruess."

Mario's heart stopped. Taking the stage were Miss Anonymous in a beautiful emerald green dress…and one of his weekend bartenders, Ken Simmons.

What the hell?

As if he weren't jealous enough of Ken, Mario had to admit that the duo did a heck of a job on the song. They even harmonized!

But what brought the two together? Were they dating? He also had to admit that Ken was brand new to the Project, so he knew little about him.

Still, what the hell?

"I wish you looked at me like you look at hhher," Laney lamented, again appearing in Mario's personal space, this time running her hand down his arm. It was quite obvious that she was tipsy…yet again.

"Laney, it's time to call it a night." Mario retorted, removing her hand from his arm, as if her touch caused combustible sparks.

One of the things that Mario did at the beginning of every Friday evening was to scan the crowd to see if his usual Uber or Lyft friends were present. He had them on speed dial as well. Earlier in the evening, he spotted Larry from Uber.

Mario let out a whistle and Larry appeared, grabbing the 20 that Mario had taken out of his wallet.

The party was over for Laney.

Chapter Four

On Sunday Buddy was ebullient as he entered the Project to begin his chopping. He seemed to embrace the day as he donned his chef's hat, a huge smile mirroring his effervescence. He was a man in love.

"Hey, Mario!" he barked loudly. "What's shaking?"

"Buddy! How was your date with Sandy?"

"Well, I am not one to kiss and tell, so let's just say it was nothing less than bitchen! We had a great time at the China Place and her house afterward. Maybe I will bring her to the man cave next time," referring to his little two-bedroom bungalow.

One of the bedrooms had been converted to a pub, with a 70-inch television and lots of couches. He had removed the closet doors, and transformed the space into a large display of every type of liquor one could image.

Buddy enquired, "How was Kickin' Karaoke?"

"Well, Miss Anonymous sang with Ken Simmons, if you can imagine that."

"Our weekend bartender?"

"One and the same. It was like their voices were meant to collaborate, they were that good. And Laney got a ride home from Larry, for the third time in as many weeks."

"Boss, you think Laney has a drinking problem? It seems that she only has a few drinks, but they really affect her."

"I think she has a drinking problem and a thinking problem, Buddy. Every time she is around me she says suggestive things, especially when she is drinking. She asked me why I didn't look at her the way I look at Miss Anonymous."

"Holy hell! Man, too bad I missed that little scene."

"It was awkward as heck, Buddy. Let's change subjects. What is Sandy's place like?"

"She has this cute little place behind the bakery. It is like this quaint little cottage straight out of *Martha Stewart Living*. And she decorated it herself."

Sandy's flair for interior design was also reflected in Sandy's Dandies, an attractive bakery with booths decorated in floral prints and tables with tablecloths that match the booths.

It was attractive and inviting. Like the woman herself, thought Buddy.

On Monday Mario called Debra Wilson to inform her that the job at the PP #2 was hers. He apologized that it took him longer than expected to make his decision, as he had interviewed three other people after his meeting with her.

She asked when she should start, and he told her that Tuesday he would meet with her at the restaurant to show her the ropes. His brother Tommy would be on hand to help.

Mario had a thought as he gathered ingredients for spaghetti and smallish meatballs for his pint-sized chefs: He ran upstairs to grab a CD and snatched up Buddy's boom box before leaving the Project.

While the kids arrived at 4:30, Mario played the song "On Top of Spaghetti," with which many were acquainted. They began to sing along, laughing and talking excitedly.

"Good afternoon, my little chefs! Let's wash up before we make our spaghetti."

Mario had the spaghetti water going and had pre-cooked sauce and meatballs, which were simmering on the stove.

"It is very important to read the directions when you cook something. This is regular spaghetti, which takes 9 to 11 minutes to cook. There is also thin spaghetti, which boils for 5 to 6 minutes because it is much thinner than regular spaghetti."

He continued, "This bowl with holes is called a colander, or a strainer. We strain the spaghetti after it is cooked and drain it really well before serving it."

Mario brought out the containers and every chef filled them with spaghetti, sauce, and meatballs.

He queried his kids: "Who can name an ingredient in this sauce?"

They all answered at once.

"Tomatoes!"

"Garlic!"

"Vegetables!"

Mario laughed. "You are all right! There are tomatoes, onions, bell peppers, garlic, carrots, celery, and spices. And, of course, mini-meatballs."

He pulled out a container of grated parmesan cheese.

"So, chefs, the author of the song 'On Top of Spaghetti,' Tom Glazer, mentions that the spaghetti is topped with cheese. Do you know what that cheese is called?"

"I know!" Emma Russo's hand shot up. "It's called parmesan, and it stinks! It reminds me of the book that my mom used to read to me called *The Stinky Cheese Man*!"

The little chefs started chattering loudly.

Mario laughed robustly. He actually was familiar with the book by Jon Scieszka, *The Stinky Cheese Man and Other Fairly Stupid Tales*, as he had read it to one of his nephews when he was babysitting. The titular tale featured the adventures of a wheel of cheese with arms and legs.

"You're right, Emma. I am going to pass around the parmesan, which is optional as a topping for your spaghetti."

Rather than sprinkle it on top of their culinary treats, the chefs all smelled it, and the looks on their faces were priceless.

"Until next time! Have a good week, everyone." Mario dismissed the class, and Joni was the last to leave, as always.

"Mr. Mario! Mr. Mario! Guess what next Monday is?"

"Gosh, Joni, I don't know what next Monday is. Tell me."

"It's my 11th birthday!"

"Well, we are going to have a celebration! What is your favorite food in the whole world, Joni?"

"Grilled cheese sandwiches and tomato soup!"

Mario portended that the temperature outside would probably hit 85 next Monday, and hardly a soup climate, but he made a promise.

"Okay! On our menu next Monday will be grilled cheese sandwiches and tomato soup!"

"Thanks, Mr. Mario, for everything." Again, Joni wrapped her tiny arms around Mario's leg.

He was smitten.

And he needed to plan a kiddie party.

Debra met Mario at the PP #2 bright and early on Tuesday morning. Tommy was also present, with a clipboard and prepared lists of employees, their phone numbers and emails; menu items; food distributors; and rules of the Project, such as a 90-minute limit on sports gatherings and birthday parties, and the limit of participants (20 kids plus parents/coaches).

Debra brought her own clipboard, and proceeded to take copious notes as Tommy and Mario spoke, a whirlwind of information swirling in her head.

An hour into Debra's orientation, a tall gentleman entered the restaurant, and the distraction was a momentary respite for her. What Buddy was to PP #1, John Ramsey was to PP #2.

"Hi there! I'm John Ramsey, chief cook the past 20 years." John served on the *Roosevelt* with Buddy, who suggested he follow him to Oakview, where they both settled in.

"Nice to meet you, John. I'm Debra Wilson." They shook hands, then she returned to Mario and Tommy.

Tommy chimed in, "So, Debra, do you have any questions?"

"Not that I can think of right now," she said. "But I can guarantee that I will in the future."

"I need to get back to PP #1, so I will let you and Tommy handle things from here." Mario asked for her phone, and punched in his number, and asked for hers.

He crossed his fingers out of reach of the others and hoped that he made the right decision in hiring Debra, his own Mystery Woman.

Back at his home Project, Mario played This Day in History with Buddy as he continued to knead some dough.

"This day in history—August 5, 1985—the establishment of the Rock and Roll Hall of Fame was announced."

"That so?"

Wait for it.

"What's a four-man rock group that makes no music? Mount Rushmore!"

Taking such pleasure in cracking himself up, Buddy let loose an enormous belly laugh before returning to his job.

By 3:00 the afternoon group had assembled. Maritza was finished with her finals, so she was free for the next three weeks, until the semester started. David was savoring his martini, and Mario and Buddy were behind the counter.

Buddy had a suggestion.

"Hey, everyone, I think we need to name our little group. How about the Mid-afternoon Mischief Makers?"

"I have another idea, which is kind of ironic," offered David. "How about the Misfits? To the outside observer, we may appear to be people from all walks of life who are just thrown together, when in reality we are diverse individuals who are all succeeding in life."

"The Misfits," Mario mused, contemplating the moniker. "I like it! Although we do occasionally make mischief. Let's vote."

The Misfits it was.

"Hey, Maritza, I almost forgot that you got mail on Friday. I have it behind the counter."

"Oh, a missive from the admirer!" burst out David gleefully upon seeing the familiar envelope. "I can't wait to see what he has come up with this time."

Mario, of course, figured out that the admirer was Bobby Wilson, but he didn't have the nerve to voice his conjecture aloud. Besides, this little game was such entertainment for the Misfits!

Maritza read aloud:

"I would call you my queen, but I have no tiara to offer you
Bring fragrant roses, but my pockets bear no coins
But I can honor you in this verse and sing a sweet song
Of my admiration which knows no bounds"

With a tear in her eye, she looked towards David, her eyebrows raised.

"I am clueless, Miss Maritza, as to the origin of this morsel of poetry. My guess is that your admirer has penned his own verse," David opined.

Maritza simply nodded, and grasped the letter to her chest.

"Bitch with a Bun is driving John crazy," announced Buddy a few days later as he entered the Project one early morning.

"Why, Buddy?"

It was 7:00 in the morning, and Mario felt a headache coming on already.

"Well, she is trying to make a lot of changes—from the menu to the placement of furniture—and he is just miserable and exhausted with it all. A few of the part-time kids quit, so she is scrambling for replacements."   Buddy was glad that he wasn't the chef at PP #2.

"Okay, I am going to go over there in a little while, after I put a pot of sauce on the stove."

At PP #2, the tables were in a different configuration, all right. John glanced toward Mario, a pained and plaintive look upon his face. He look sleep-deprived, to top it all off.

"How are things going over here?"

Debra was out of reach.

"Boss, you've gotta put a stop to Debra's behavior! She is upsetting everyone with her desire to make changes. One of our hallmarks as a restaurant is that we bring the customers what they want, not what the staff wants. Plus, the college kids are dropping like flies!"

"Okay, John. Let me have a chat with Debra. Thanks for hanging in there."

Mario had enough on his plate without having to deal with a pain-in-the-butt new manager.

He spotted Debra in the break room.

"Debra, give me a report card on your first two weeks at PP #2." Mario cut to the chase, anxious to get back to his dough and floured fingers.

"Well, I would say that things are going fairly well. A few of the college kids quit, but I have distributed some applications in the past few days that I hope will bring some good results."

Debra looked down as she gave the verbal report card, without revealing the grade that she would ascribe to her performance.

"Just let me know if you are planning on making any changes, to the menu or otherwise. We need to be on the same page with our sister restaurants." Mario tried to be firm while continuing to show her the ropes.

"Mario, I was thinking of adding eggplant parmesan to the menu, as a vegetarian option. What do you think?"

Mario's headache grew stronger, as a faint throbbing began. If he had no aspirin at PP #1, he was going to have to dispatch Buddy to the Dollar Bonanza to fetch some.

"Debra, I think that is a negative. We don't even offer eggplant as a topping for our pizza, as some pizza parlors do. As for non-meat items, we have salad, cheese ravioli, tons of pizza toppings, and fettuccine alfredo. Tell you what: Let's explore some other vegan or vegetarian offerings when we have a chance to sit down and chat. For now, we need to get back to work."

Debra seemed appeased, if only temporarily.

Mario was grateful to return to his Project, his safe space.

In the early afternoon, Laney popped in, a guilty look on her face.

"I'm so sorry, Mario. I behaved horribly."

"Listen, Laney, I think that the apology tour needs to come to a screeching stop. You need to reflect on your behavior when you are drinking. I sincerely think that you need help."

"Well, I don't know if that is true, but I am sorry. I brought over a preview copy of the Book of Excellence, and I wanted to congratulate you." With that, she handed him a thick tome peppered with the very best places and services in the city of Oakview. And she turned to leave.

Mario summoned Buddy before opening to the Best Italian Restaurant section.

"Wa-hoo, Mario! There you have it—numbers one and two, PP #1 and PP #2! And, as usual, Primavera came in third. Wonder how Gina Toledo feels about that one." Buddy was referring to the owner of Primavera.

When it was break time, Buddy decided to go back to Dollar Bonanza.

"I need more balloons, as the ones from a few weeks ago have deflated. And I need more thank-you pencils. Need anything, Mario?"

"Yeah, get me some aspirin, please." He handed a five-dollar bill to Buddy.

Later that afternoon, there was an impromptu celebration when the Misfits gathered.

Once David had his martini, Mario made a little speech:

"Okay, Misfits. I have an announcement to make. Laney stopped by with an advance copy of the Book of Excellence, and PP #1 and PP #2 came in first and second, for the third year in a row!" He tossed the book on to the table where David was sitting, and everyone scrambled to see it.

The four went crazy, all speaking at once. Some of them were actually in the pictures of the restaurant that Laney included in the book.

"Guys, guys. I think we need to brainstorm for a way to give back to the Oakview community for voting for us. Does anyone have any ideas?" Mario queried the Misfits.

"How about half-price mini pizzas for just a few hours on one day only?"   It was Buddy's turn to chime in.

"I think that's a wonderful idea!" offered Maritza. "What would be a good day for our little celebration?"

"We need to discuss preparations," Mario noted. "For example, we should spend a few days beforehand to assemble mini boxes. And we should order extra food from our distributors. And we need a catchy name for whatever day it is."

"How about 'Three-Dollar Thank-You Thursday'?" asked David. "It is simple and to the point, to say nothing of alliterative! And the three stands for back-to-back-to-back victories."

"That sounds great, David!" Mario smiled broadly at the group. "Today is Tuesday, so we have two days until our sale. I will stop by the *Register* and arrange an ad for Wednesday's and Thursday's papers, and we can start constructing boxes."

To the group, he added: "I want to thank you for all of the work you have done this past year, from in the kitchen (he smiled at Buddy), to the front counter (smiles for Maritza) to moral support (he acknowledged David). This is a celebration for the community, and for the Misfits!"

"To the Misfits!" David raised his martini glass.

On Thursday, from 1:00 to 3:00, Three-Dollar Thank-You Thursday brought in Oakviewites in droves. It was as if the crowd from Kickin' Karaoke appeared one day early, and the pizza boxes literally stacked to the ceiling in multiple rows seemed to disappear.

The rules were simple: Only to-go orders and no drinks. Just pepperoni and cheese mini pizzas. No more than three per customer.

Debra closed down PP #2 and was instrumental in crowd control.

Pizza boxes flew off the shelves, and pies were in and out of the pizza ovens in less than five minutes. When things calmed down, Mario would figure out just how many pies were sold.

Everyone worked together to make Three-Dollar Thank-You Thursday a success. Even David donned an apron and started pizza-making when things got intense.

When Buddy inquired about David's culinary skills, David reassured him that he was a seasoned cook.

"My undergraduate years were punctuated by stints working in the LaFortune Student Center at Notre Dame. I spent many an hour crafting pizzas for my fellow students," said David.

By 2:30, every last bit of dough and sauce had disappeared. Maritza placed a sold-out sign on the door. Closed for the rest of today.

Debra returned to PP #2.

The Misfits collapsed, draping themselves over chairs and booths, every last bit of strength sapped from their collective bodies.

"Whose cockamamie idea was this?" Buddy barked, the exhaustion getting the better of him.

Mario addressed the Misfits.

"Listen, we did what we set out to do: to thank the community for their votes. I know we all worked really hard today, and the Project is closed for the rest of the day and evening. I will call those who are scheduled to come in for the second shift. For now, everyone go home and take pride in what you have done today for the community. Thank you all so much."

When everyone left, and he had made the necessary calls, Mario took his ten-step commute and, diving onto his bed, slept like the dead for 12 hours straight.

Chapter Five

If the inferno had not wrought such a devastating annihilation, one might have labeled it beautiful.

It was as if Mother Nature had dipped into the autumnal colors in a box of 64 Crayola Crayons and picked out the most vibrant hues--burnt orange, neon carrot, goldenrod, and scarlet—to craft the prolific flames that seemed to touch their tips to the jet-black sky.

It was nearing midnight when alarms and sirens began to wake the citizens of Oakview, especially those who lived off Main Street.

And, in the moments that followed, Sandy Charles learned the meaning of "three-alarm fire" as she watched her precious Sandy's Dandies burn to the ground.

Three firehouses responded to the conflagration: Oakview, Glendale, and Mount Olive. Thus, the term applies to three alarms.

Smoke infiltrated the majority of Main Street as Sandy stood shivering from the cold and wrapped in a blanket. Tears freely flowed as she saw her beloved bakery collapse onto itself, raining sparks over the building and over her cottage, which the firemen miraculously saved. Luckily, no other businesses or homes were touched.

Buddy flew to the scene once he saw the alert on his phone. Since his Navy stint he had become a light sleeper, as sailors had to be at the ready for anything that transpired, in the day or nighttime.

He rushed to Sandy, who stood on the other side of Main. Scooping her up in his arms he whispered to her, "Oh, darlin'! It will be okay. I am here for you."

Neighbors appeared in pajamas and blankets, and all assembled around Sandy, whose heartbreak was reflected in her red-stained eyes and continuous stream of tears.

She learned hours later that the cause of the fire was electrical. She had kept an antique oven from her father in the bakery, but rarely used it. It was a symbol of his legacy to Sandy, as he started the bakery under the name Dan's Delights. Her parents had passed away years ago, after gifting the bakery to her. She had no siblings to cling to in her heartbreaking distress.

A fireman informed Sandy that the culprit was a mouse, found dead at the scene after presumably chewing on the electrical cord of the oven. The cord was probably already frayed, he explained.

Because tenting a building often scatters critters in all directions, the mouse most likely was fleeing from the offices of Mayor Max next door, who was remodeling. The renovation would include a glassed-in room off Max's office for his son EJ. Max figured that that would be a better alternative to having a playpen in the area where he conducted business.

"Oh, Buddy! I shouldn't have kept the oven plugged in! I rarely used it. Look what I've done!" Sandy was beside herself with guilt and torment.

"Darlin', don't blame yourself. I have an idea: Why don't you come and stay at the man cave with me, since your home is not habitable yet? I have two bedrooms, and I can stay in the pub. I have a pull-out couch."

Sandy could barely think. Her mind was filled with what ifs and what will bes, swirling around her exhaustion and disbelief.

"Okay," she said finally, her voice small and weak, her mind resolved to comply. She really had no other choice, with no other family in the area.

After most of the firemen left, and the Oakviewites returned to their homes and beds, Buddy and Sandy walked the three blocks to his house after retrieving some clothes from her smoke-filled cottage.

Thankfully, it was a Monday, and Buddy had time to spend with Sandy. He hoped that she might sleep for a few hours.

Sandy helped Buddy change the sheets on his bed, and he went into the pub to pour her a small glass of brandy.

"This might help you sleep, honey," he said, placing it on the nightstand. "If you need anything, just come get me in the pub. I'm just a wall away."

With that, he gently kissed her forehead and left to grab some sleep himself.

At 4:30 in the morning, he was awakened by soft sobbing from his bedroom. He dashed out of bed and knocked on the door.

Sandy welcomed him, her frail voice barely audible. "Come in, Buddy."

"Oh, darlin'! I feel so sad to see you in this predicament. But, just think: You will be able to rebuild the bakery and make it however you want it to be. Heck, you can expand it, or add a second floor. You will be like one of those birds coming up from a fire!"

"A phoenix rising from the ashes. That is so sweet, Buddy.   I wish that I had your positive attitude about all of this, but I am completely heartbroken. Would you mind holding me for a while? "

"Sure thing, honey."

Tenderly, Buddy put his arm around Sandy and stroked her arm, his gentle whispers summoning her to rest. Within minutes, she was asleep, but he took his time leaving her side, and instead reveled in the sweetness of her soft breathing until he, too, had dozed off.

When she awoke, Sandy took a moment to realize where she was. And the house looked so different in the daylight.

It was, indeed, a man cave, decorated in masculine colors of navy blue and brown. It was a tidy place, surprisingly. Buddy had done a wonderful job in making the cottage his own.

He awakened with a huge smile on his face.

"Well, good morning, honey! Guess I dozed off before I could move to my own bed. How are you doing this morning?"

"Just fine, Buddy. Just fine."

She glanced at the clock.

"Buddy! It's 11:30 in the morning! I have never slept this late in my entire life!"

"Well, you needed the rest, darlin'. Now you need some breakfast. What's your poison? I have eggs, bacon, sausage, and hash browns."

"How about all of the above?" Sandy asked sheepishly. She was starving after the chaos and mental and physical exhaustion. Sleep had been her salvation.

"Great! Would you like to shower while I cook?"

Buddy turned on his home boom box to KFUNN radio. When "Build Me Up Buttercup" came on, he sang loudly and a bit off-key.

He had to laugh. Mario once told him to not quit his day job when he was warbling to one of his beloved '70s hits. But he always sang with such gusto, and always enjoyed himself.

And he used the microphone at Kickin' Karaoke for emcee purposes only, never for singing.

After a leisurely breakfast, Buddy accompanied Sandy to her property. An insurance adjuster surveyed the damage, and Sandy scanned the charred ruins for anything she might salvage. The next day, a demolition crew would begin razing the remains of the property and clearing out the debris.

It was a grueling, hours-long exercise, and Buddy had a plan after they walked away from the destruction.

"Why don't we go bowling? We need to do something fun today. You deserve it after all you've been through."

"Oh, Buddy, what a wonderful idea!"

And it was. They had lots of fun competing for first place at Smashing Pins, and both agreed that the bowling alley food was the ultimate in comfort food and surprisingly good. Burgers, chili and cornbread, mac and cheese. Add a beer, and your meal was complete.

Sandy beat Buddy, two games to one.

There was much excitement when one of the bowlers got a perfect game, and a photographer and reporter from the *Oakview Tribune* were dispatched to take photos and jot down some details for the next day's paper.

Buddy photobombed just for the heck of it, and the photographer placed her hands on her hips and just glared at him.

He quickly retreated, and he and Sandy left the bowling alley laughing.

They walked the five blocks to Buddy's house, and when they arrived, Sandy had only one calming thought: She felt at home.

Mario loaded up on balloons and streamers and got to the Boys and Girls Club an hour before he usually arrived. He set the decorations in the kitchen and set out bowls of tomato soup which he had already made and chilled. Today, his students would be making the cheese sandwiches and decorating the labels for the tip cans for Taste of Oakview.

Joni was the first to arrive.

She looked so adorable in her red sundress with bows atop her curly hair, not in pigtails today.

"Happy birthday, Joni!" Mario bent down to give her a proper hug. "Have you had a good day so far?"

"Yes, it has been lots of fun! My grandmother took me to the diner for breakfast and we both made my birthday cake. It is white with chocolate frosting!!"

"Wow, that sounds delicious!" Mario wished that he could indulge in a piece himself.

After the students came in and had washed up, Mario began his instructions.

"Good afternoon, my little chefs! Today we are celebrating Joni on her 11th birthday. Does anyone else have a birthday this month?"

No one waved their hand.

"Okay, I have a suggestion: We should have a birthday celebration once a month for all of those who share birthdays that month. Please fill in this blank calendar with your name on your birth date before you leave today. But let's first make some sandwiches."

Mario instructed the students on the proper way to grill a cheese sandwich, pointing out the different cheese possibilities. He grilled all of their sandwiches on a big grill pan; he didn't trust them with the stove just yet.

Once the sandwiches were made and wrapped, he doled out crayons to the group, along with the labels that had Oakview Boys and Girls Club printed at the bottom.

"Okay, chefs. As you know, a Taste of Oakview brings all of the businesses in the town together for an evening of tasting little tidbits of food. Instead of the business owners getting tips, the tips will go to this club for sports equipment and other programs."

He concluded, "I would like you to decorate a label with your thanks to the community for their tips."

After the labels were finished, all of the students grabbed a bag and put in soup, a sandwich, and a cupcake, which Mario commissioned Sandy to bake.

In robust tones, the group sang "Happy Birthday" to Joni, then exited the club.

When the students were gone, Joni placed her arms around Mario's leg and whispered, "I love you, Mr. Mario."

He didn't think his heart could contain all of the joy that he was feeling.

It was early in the morning and the sun burnt bright, a harbinger of the scorching temperatures that would inevitably follow over the course of the day.

August was passing quickly. Soon, students would return en masse to Oakview Elementary School, Bennington High School and Walker College.

There were only two Fridays left for Kickin' Karaoke. Miss Anonymous had been absent the past two Fridays, much to the dismay of Mario, who anticipated the return of his Karaoke Angel. He spent many nights thinking of her and hoping to find her in his dreams.

"So, Buddy, how are you and your roommate getting along?" Mario had to tease his pal on Tuesday. "Are you playing house together nicely?"

Snicker, snicker.

"Let's just say that life is fine, Mario! I know that Sandy will return to her cottage soon, so I am just enjoying our time together."

He had a thought.

"Hey, we haven't played This Day in History for a while! Guess what today is, Mario?"

"I have no idea, Buddy."

"August 21, 1959: Hawaii becomes the 50th US state."

Just wait for the joke du jour…

"What did an advertisement for Maui say?"

"What did it say?" asked Mario.

"Don't worry. Beach happy!"

"Bet you thought I would be telling a joke about getting lei'd! Fooled ya!"

Chuckling, Buddy went back to making sauce.

And thought about getting laid—using a different spelling.

On Friday night Steve and Mario caught up in between tending bar.

"Hey, how are the wedding plans coming along?" Mario asked, his hands skillfully maneuvering two nozzles, one emitting gin, and the other, tonic water.

"Well, the date is set for December 15 at Oakview Christian Church. The reception will be at Primavera," said Steve as he rimmed a margarita glass with coarse salt.

"Why not here?" Mario was kind of hoping he could host the soiree.

"I wanted to give my best man a break! I just want you to enjoy yourself for one day. You deserve it."

"Thanks, Steve. I just need to conjure a plus one to enjoy it even more, but I don't think even the most adept magician can accomplish that feat."

Mario needed to step up his romance game. And soon.

Just as he was pondering the possibilities, Miss Anonymous took to the stage.

His heart skipped a beat. He had felt her absence deeply the past two weeks, and he was grateful for her return.

"Ladies and gentlemen, let's hear it for our next performer," shouted Buddy, turning toward her and assisting her up the stage.

The powerful lyrics of Gloria Gaynor's "I Will Survive" proved a fitting anthem for Miss Anonymous, who, unknown as yet to others in the audience, had endured heartache and had come back all the better for it. She sang with unbridled passion, like the lyrics were meant for her and her backstory.

Mario stopped to gaze at his Karaoke Angel, who had donned a floral dress which touched on her femininity. Her hair shone in the light, straight tonight instead of in her usual cascade of curls. She had secured half of it in a beautiful floral barrette, matching the flowers of her dress. She was the epitome of a lady--an exquisite, beautiful creation sent from above.

The crowd swayed and sang along, and the thunderous applause filled the room as she departed the Project, alone once again.

And, once again, she escaped with her secrets and stories intact.

Monday morning brought all kinds of challenges for Mario, as Mondays are wont to do.

The distributor had delivered boxes of tomatoes on Sunday, and, as he was about to open one of them, a nasty smell wafted out: Many of the tomatoes were rotten.

They say that one bad apple doesn't spoil the whole bunch, but one bad tomato seemed to.

"Hey, Buddy, I am going to drive down to PP #2 and see if Debra has any extra tomatoes," he shouted back to the kitchen.

"Sure thing, Boss. You say hi to John for me, okay?"

Mario made a note to ask John how things were, when all of a sudden Maisie barged into the restaurant.

"Mario! Mario! I chased away the homeless guy again! Right in front of my door!"

"Maisie, I need to go to the other restaurant. I promise I will look into it when I get back."

"But Mario!"

"I'm sorry, Maisie, but I have to go."

At PP #2, John and Debra seemed to be having it out. The subject? Oregano.

"I really think that you need to add more oregano to your sauce," demanded Debra. "It needs a little punch."

"But Debra, this recipe is tried and true. Customers are used to it tasting the way it does. I say if it ain't broke, don't fix it!"

"What is going on here?" asked Mario. "Debra, I thought that we agreed to discuss any changes before they become, well, changes."

"This is just a small change, Mario. I suggested that John add more oregano to his sauce."

"No can do, Debra. The recipe is sacrosanct. We have used the same recipe for the past 50 years, and it will never change."

With that, Mario went into the back room of the restaurant to fetch tomatoes, and then left. He didn't wait for a reply from Debra.

He only had one thought: Where did he put the aspirin from Dollar Bonanza?

At Hope Inn, Porter and Bobby were tossing a baseball in the front yard and solving the problems of the world. Or, at least, their worlds.

"How is everything with Sophia?" asked Bobby, referring to Porter's girlfriend Sophia Bennington.

"Real good. She's just busy with ASB stuff. In two weeks, her family leaves for their summer vacation in San Diego. I am going to try to spend as much time with her as I can, in between practices. And we have baseball camp for little kids next week. Any luck with Maritza?"

"I have sent her eight anonymous letters with verses of poetry. I think that it is time to come clean and reveal myself. But I have a plan: I am going to have her go on a scavenger hunt! I need to really plan this out, and I am going to enlist some people in town to help out," said Bobby. He was a man with a mission.

"That sounds really cool!" said Porter. "Let me know if you need any help."

Alone in his room that evening, Bobby started to chart his course for the hunt. He felt like a detective in a spy novel, cleverly piecing together clues to a mystery meant for only one person.

Too bad his plan would have to be put on ice for a while.

Chapter Six

So Long Summer weekend was upon Oakview as August was about to bow to September and usher in the hottest temperatures all season.

Carnival rides were erected mid-week, the eager eyes of children longingly marking the days until Friday. Along the midway would be games such as the Bean Bag Toss and Balloon Pop, and there would be deep fried offerings such as funnel cakes and loaded tots with bacon and cheese.

Stomach-churning rides like the Zipper and Gravitron will thrill the teenagers while little ones sit atop ponies and marvel at the petting zoo.

To officially kick off the festivities, Mayor Max took to the microphone in the town square Friday afternoon, Oakviewites congregating around him.

"My dear citizens of Oakview, it has been a wonderful summer season, punctuated by good times and bad, but through it all, we have grown as a community. We are lucky to live in a town where our citizens are caring, giving people. With that in mind, I thank you in advance for your donations to the Boys and Girls Club as you experience a Taste of Oakview tomorrow night."

With a flourish, Max raised both arms in the air and shouted, "Ladies and gentlemen, welcome to So Long Summer!" He exclaimed the start of the end-of-summer bash as the audience clapped boisterously and scattered to enjoy the last glorious days before fall—and all of its responsibilities—set in.

Because of the celebration, Kickin' Karaoke was postponed until next Friday, the final performances to delight the throngs that would inevitably gather.

Saturday night brought in a plethora of pop-up tents, as business owners set up shop on the now-closed Main Street with their delicious offerings.

Mayor Max was always challenged to manufacture something delectable, and this year he really came through with the sweet and the savory—mini muffins and mini quiches.

Mario, in collaboration with Debra, chose a menu of mini meatballs, toasted ravioli with marinara, and small slices of garlic bread. Together, they divvied up the cooking and were at the ready with overflowing chafing dishes.

"Mario, this is really fabulous!" Debra was exuberant at the numbers of Oakviewites that flooded the town square and enjoyed samples for a good cause. She was unaccustomed to small-town life after living in Chicago before landing in Oakview.

She had quickly come to love this town and its residents and was so grateful for this second chance for herself and Bobby.

David happened by, but spent most of his evening with Gloria, even helping to serve small cups of cream of chicken soup and mini ham and cheese sandwiches on sourdough bread.

When the food ran out, each vendor called it a night but left the tents up for the next day. There was no need to worry about their being stolen in this town that, as Mayor Max attested, was a caring community.

Coincidentally, Debra and Mario closed up at the same time that Gloria and David did.

"Ladies, may I accompany you back to the inn?" David asked.

The three set out on this lovely evening, the lights in the town square twinkling brightly as if to wink good night to the walkers.

"My, what an evening!" David, too, was enamored with So Long Summer. He gushed, "This event really displayed the heart of this quaint little town. I assume that lots of money was made for the tots at the Boys and Girls Club."

"Yes!" Debra was quick to supply an answer. "Mario had to empty our can twice because it was overflowing! The children who frequent the Club will enjoy more programs and sports equipment."

As they approached the inn, with all of its windows open on this balmy night, Debra and David said the same thing in unison:

"Uh-oh!" they exclaimed.

Gloria was perplexed.

"What do you mean by uh-oh?" she asked.

"Well," said David, "that aroma wafting about the inn provided a pungent backdrop for many an evening during my undergraduate years at Notre Dame."

"I am sorry, but I have no idea what you are taking about!" Poor Gloria was beside herself at this point.

The three followed the trail of the scent to the pool that sits between the inn and the Sheffields' bungalow.

"Oh, we thought you'd be home much later," said Porter, reclining lazily in a chaise lounge.

"Well, we are here and this soiree is over," declared David, grabbing the joint out of Bobby's hand.

"Hey! You're harsh-ing my marsh-mal-low!" Bobby declared slowly, as if enunciating every syllable could hide the effects of the marijuana.

David contained a grin. "I think you mean harshing your mellow."

"Yeah, that." Bobby agreed.

Gloria was in tears, and Debra was fit to be tied. They both cited the fact that the tokers were athletes who should be avoiding anything harmful to their bodies, not partaking of it. Porter confessed that he got the joint from a teammate.

The punishments were strict: No leaving the house except for practice, no cell phones for a week, and they were to spend their days working at either the inn or PP #2, doing whatever chores were necessary.

The boys slumped off to their rooms and David quickly got rid of the evidence.

About an hour later, Gloria found sleep an impossibility and decided to spend some time in the parlor, her place of solace.

She was surprised to find David there, a glass of red wine in his hand.

"Hello, Gloria," he stood to welcome her. "Would you like a glass of cabernet sauvignon?"

"Yes, thanks so much. I could use that about now."

Neither spoke in the moments that followed.

Finally, David tried to offer some measure of comfort.

"I guess we can attribute tonight's transgression to the adage of boys will be boys, but I know that isn't much of a consolation for you," he said.

Gloria took a sip of her wine, and contemplated a response.

"My ex-husband turned out to be a drug addict and drugs were the last thing that I would ever think Porter would involve himself with."

Tears began to flow softly as she said, "It is hard to be both mother and father to a young adult male."

David offered his handkerchief to Gloria, a gesture that surprised her and comforted her at the same time. Who carries a handkerchief these days?

"I know it must be a huge responsibility. But I know this much: You are doing a great job with Porter. He is a fine young man with lofty goals and manners befitting a gentleman."

David's pronouncement made Gloria cry even more.

He took her wine and placed it on the coffee table and went to sit next to her, putting his arm around her. Initially she stiffened, then she relaxed and gave in to the warmth that his body offered in abundance. It had been a long time since she lavished in the arms of a man, and it felt so good.

They sat there for a long time, in companionable silence. No words were necessary. The silence spoke for itself.

"So, Maritza, what do you hear from your secret admirer these days?" Mario inquired a few days later. "Any more poetry?"

"Mario! It has been weeks since his last letter! I think he forgot about me!"

The dejected look on Maritza's pretty face said volumes about her disappointment. She was becoming accustomed to the little gifts of verse and looked forward to coming to work even more than she usually did.

"Well, I am sure that you will hear from him soon." Mario reassured her. But he, too, wondered if the excitement had vanquished.

The buzz in the Project was mostly about the success of So Long Summer, which netted $2,500 for the Boys and Girls Club.

Mario missed his usual Monday gig there because the whole town was pitching in to clean up Main Street. Next week, for sure.

Chief Stanley popped in and requested a private chat with Mario, so they retreated into the break room. Buddy locked eyes with Mario and his brows arched high, as if to question what the heck is up. Mario raised his shoulders and looked skeptical.

"So, Mario, I got a call this afternoon from the California Institution for Men. Scott Williams will be set free tomorrow."

Mario simply stared at Bryan, collecting his thoughts.

"Bryan, thanks for the head's up, but I don't think he would have the audacity to show up here, let alone in Oakview."

"Let's hope so," Bryan said, trying to convince Mario— and himself.

David stopped in the next day, eager to start a Scrabble game with Mario. The score was tied 6-6 for games won, so the competition had become heated.

They actually got in half of a game before David's daughter came in with her administrative assistant.

"Game!" yelled Mario. "Ha, ha! I'm ahead, 7-6!"

"Drat!" exclaimed David. "I was just about to make a play with the word finesse!" He chuckled.

He hugged the ladies and Mario brought their wine.

"Hi Sis! Hi Ellie!" said Mario, planting a kiss on Cassie's cheek.

"Hey, little brother!" she replied, then turned to her father.

"So, Dad, I wanted to ask you something," said Cassie. "Ellie and I were calendaring for the school year, and I thought that you would be an excellent judge for Poetry Comes Alive."

She said it! She just matter-of-factly said *Dad!*

Ellie and David just smiled at each another.

"Pray, tell, what is Poetry Comes Alive?" David was perplexed.

"It's a national competition, with one winner for every state, and each state submits one poet. It starts at the county level, after the school competition."

She continued, "I have been the moderator for the event the past four years, and every year the moderator at Bristol Academy has had the first-place winners for our county. Marilyn James is a very nice person, but she must run a really tight ship at Bristol."

"I'd be delighted to be a judge! Just let me know the date."

Cassie went on to explain how the students memorize poems on the PCA website, and are judged on their accuracy and performance.

And she didn't even realize how she addressed him.

Buddy and Sandy had established a comfortable routine: He brought home food for dinner every day, and she baked bread and desserts.

She was given the green light to move back into her cottage, but she wasn't ready yet. She was happy at Buddy's, for the most part. But she was getting bored and on edge, not having a job to go to every day.

Lately, Buddy had sensed this restlessness in Sandy. He decided to address it after dinner one evening.

"Darlin', is everything okay with you? You seem out of sorts of late and not yourself."

"The truth is, Buddy, I am bothered by two things, and I am hoping you can help me with both of them."

"Sure, honey, just say the word and I am yours."

"Well, I really miss going to work, and I was wondering if I might go to the Pizza Project a few hours a day and make desserts and coffee. I know that people really miss sweet treats from my bakery, and I know how to make some Italian goodies, like tiramisu, cannolis, and crostata. What do you think? What would Mario say?"

"Darlin', it's a fabulous idea! You can get out of the house and do what you do best. And Oakviewites will be happy campers again! I will ask Mario tomorrow."

"Oh, Buddy, thank you so much! You don't know what this means to me."

"What is the other thing, honey?"

"Buddy, I have enjoyed the closeness that we have shared since I came to live here. I don't know how to ask you this next favor."

She stood up and composed her words carefully.

"I wanted to ask you to make love with me, but I didn't know how. You know that Steve Carrell movie about his being a virgin?"

Buddy thought a bit.

"Yes, *The 40-Year-Old Virgin*," he said, then quickly did a double-take.

"You're a 40-year-old virgin?!!" Buddy asked incredulously.

"42," Sandy said softly, looking down at the floor.

That evening, instead of sleeping in the pub on his pull-out couch, Buddy joined Sandy in his bedroom, in his huge king-sized bed.

With all of the tenderness within him, Buddy kissed Sandy gently at first, traversing her face and her chest before undressing her. He never stopped kissing her as he shed her blouse, skirt, and underwear.

When he touched her breast for the first time, she shivered, but it had nothing to do with the cold on this steamy September night.

As she lay there naked, he just had one word for her, which he whispered softly to her: "Beautiful. Simply beautiful."

Sandy followed suit in undressing Buddy, as she explored his body with her willing hands, marveling at the wonder of it as if she had found buried treasure that somehow had been lost to her. She couldn't get enough.

As they lay spent in the aftermath of lovemaking, she repeated what she had said previously:

"You don't know what this means to me."

Chapter Seven

Maisie had had enough of the homeless man who seemed to like camping out at her front door. She came in through the cleaners' back entrance and grabbed a broom to shoo him away.

"Young man, why are you darkening my doorstep night after night?" she demanded, the broom at the ready for an attack as she opened the front door.

"I am sorry, ma'am, but your door is set far back, making for a more shielded space from the night cold. I will be moving along now." With that, he rolled up his sleeping bag and gathered his meager belongings: a worn backpack, a blanket, and a thin, threadbare jacket.

"Where do you go after leaving here every morning?" Maisie was curious, but stayed at a safe distance.

"Well, I go to the park, the museum, or the petting zoo. My choices are endless. I try to scare up some food along the way."

As he set out on his uncertain journey, Maisie dashed inside and grabbed her day's lunch.

"Here, young man," she said, flying after him. "Take this. At least you will know where one meal is coming from today."

"I appreciate it, ma'am. I am most grateful."

Maisie watched him slowly traverse Main Street, grasping the bag as if it were filled with gold. She said a prayer of thanks for the abundant blessings in her life the past 70 years.

The final evening of Kickin' Karaoke had brought most of the town to the Pizza Project, and Buddy was poised for a good time.

Mario had put two and two together and teased Buddy earlier in the week when Buddy seemed to be walking on air.

"No kissing and telling!" bellowed Buddy, honoring the promise to himself that he established many years ago. He had much respect for his lady loves.

He had a thought as he was setting up his stage for the host of singers already slated to perform.

"Hey, boss, I won't be here tomorrow to play This Day in History, so we will have to play today and pretend it's tomorrow," Buddy said.

"Okay, lay it on me, Buddy," Mario replied.

"The Saturday before Labor Day, which is tomorrow, is International Bacon Day. It was established in 2004 by a group of students at the University of Colorado at Boulder."

"Oh, really?"

"In honor of such a prestigious day, I bring you the joke du jour. What did Mr. Piglet say to Mrs. Piglet when she was bugging the heck out of him?"

"I don't know," said Mario.

"You're bacon me crazy!"

Buddy guffawed loudly, raising the eyebrows of some early birds who were enjoying some lasagna and pepperoni pizza, favorites of Project regulars. They were the smart ones, securing a table on what would become the most crowded evening all summer.

Sandy was enjoying her first time in Mario's kitchen, baking Italian treats for those who wished to cap off their meal with coffee and something sweet.

By 6:00, the place was overflowing. Mario had extra bartenders on hand, and he enlisted the help of his brother Billy and sister Sadie to help serve.

Buddy took to the stage.

"Hey, everyone! It has been my pleasure to emcee Kickin' Karaoke all summer. Thanks to all of you brave souls who shared your musical talents with the whole town. Look for karaoke to return next May for another great summer of tunes and talent!"

"Please give it up for our first performers, Harley and Mayor Max!" he bellowed.

The married duo performed "Lucky" by Jason Mraz and Colbie Caillat, a pertinent song for a couple so much in love with each other, their son, and their life.

Surprisingly, Laney took her turn at karaoke for the first time, belting out "Let It Go" from the Disney movie *Frozen*. Perhaps that provided a harbinger of change for Laney, prompting her to let go of the past and move forward. She appeared sober and serious, but heartfelt.

As always, Miss Anonymous preferred to be last on the list.

Tonight, she enlisted the help of Ken Simmons with their rendition of "Don't Go Breakin' My Heart" by Elton John and Kiki Dee. It was a perfect karaoke duet, and they did a great job in their performance.

When they were finished, Mario rushed over to Miss Anonymous and put his hand out to shake hers. But, in a twist, he placed a kiss over her hand and passed something to her.

"Thank you for gracing us with your lovely presence this summer," he said. "You have a beautiful voice which was like a gift to this whole community."

He continued, "Here is my card, in case you ever need me. My cell phone number is on the back."

They were interrupted by Sandy, who looked from Miss Anonymous to Mario and stammered, "I am so sorry to bother you, but Mario, you are needed in the kitchen immediately!"

"Excuse me," Mario grudgingly said. And Miss Anonymous took her leave.

Mario stopped in his tracks when he entered the kitchen, horrified at what he saw.

"What in the hell happened? And why are you here?"

He was staring at the bloody face of Scott Williams, fresh out of prison and, apparently, already in deep trouble.

Laney, who was in the kitchen assisting Sandy, had gathered towels, attempting to clean up the wound.

"I have helped with a lot of accidents in the plant over the years, so I am a seasoned pro," Sandy assured Mario.

"I came to apologize to you," began Scott, "and some jerk blindsided me in the alley with a sucker punch and I face-planted onto the asphalt. I snuck in the back door so as not to frighten your guests. I never saw the guy's face, but his words were very clear: This one's for Mario."

"Holy shit!" exclaimed Buddy as he joined the kitchen crowd that was ever growing. Thankfully, most of the karaoke crowd had left for the evening.

Scott looked to Mario. Bravely, and with all of those onlookers listening, he continued.

"Did you know that there are twelve-step programs in prison? I joined Gamblers' Anonymous at Chino. One of the steps is to make amends to those you have harmed, and that's why I'm here. I am sorry to all of you that I have hurt."

Suddenly, Laney's eyes filled with tears. She continued to nurse Scott with a gentle hand. It felt good to reach out to someone who really needed help and to abandon her own selfish desires.

When the commotion had died down, and everyone was gone except for Laney, Mario, Scott and Chief Stanley, Laney invited Scott to her house, where he continued to heal. And she began to heal as well.

The Two Tokers had quite the punitive week. At the inn, they mopped floors, scrubbed toilets, and changed sheets. They even learned how to make chocolate-chip scones and French bread.

Gloria figured that the skills she introduced to Porter and Bobby might serve them well in college and beyond. David dubbed them "life skills."

At PP #2, they took inventory after deliveries, learned how to make pizza, and doubled as cooks and servers.

With their cell phones safely back in their hands, they didn't know whom to text or call first. The freedom was immeasurable.

Bobby was finally able to craft his scavenger hunt. He had spoken to key people in town, and left little clues with them that Maritza was to pick up.

Now, he had to pen his letter.

Dear Maritza,

This is your secret admirer, sending you this last letter. It is time to reveal my identity to you.

I have devised a scavenger hunt for you to complete on Monday, your day off from school and work. Please begin at the cleaners at 11:30. I will meet you at 12:00 at the Walker College student union.

I will be the one with a dozen red roses.

Me

Bobby ran the letter over to the Pizza Project that evening and placed it in the mailbox. Only three days until Monday, and Maritza's big surprise.

The next day, Maritza shared the letter with the Misfits.

"Oh, how clever!" proclaimed David, who like the others, expressed a desire to join in on the hunt.

"You guys, no!" exclaimed Maritza. "Don't you dare show up at the student union on Monday!! I would be totally embarrassed!"

"Don't worry, honey," assured Buddy. "We were just yanking your chain.   We are all just as excited as you are to know the identity of your secret admirer."

"Well, I will give you a full report on Tuesday," said Maritza.

At 11:30 promptly, Maritza showed up at the Oakview Cleaners. Maisie greeted her in her own grouchy way.

"So, you have a secret admirer, I understand," she said. "Here, this is for you."

Hello Maritza,

This first clue will reveal my passion and my zeal
It is how I spend my time when I'm not making rhymes

With that, Maisie produced a tiny plastic football with a message attached, saying that her next stop is the *Oakview Register*.

Maritza was intrigued.

At the *Register*, Coco, the receptionist, smiled widely when Maritza entered the room.

"Oh, honey! I am so excited to be in on this little adventure! Here is your letter!" said Coco exuberantly.

This next clue is yummy and for the tummy
It is my favorite stuff of which I cannot get enough

Coco passed her a small plastic piece of pizza, with a message to go to Main Street Treasures, Sabrina Patterson's boutique.

Like Coco, Sabrina was pleased to be in on the clue-gathering.

"Maritza! I have been waiting for you! Here is your next clue." Sabrina handed her the letter.

This is where I will hover when the month is over
I will be a newbie, not like you'll be

The clue was a bookmark from the Walker College bookstore, with a note to move on to the Oakview National Bank, where Mayor Max's husband Harley was the manager.

Jeff, the receptionist, was glad to hand over Maritza's final clue.

This clue is last and I've had a blast
Make your way on over where you'll discover
My true identity at last

With that, Jeff handed Maritza one beautiful red rose.

It wasn't hard to spot Bobby in the student union. He was the only person carrying a bouquet of roses and the goofiest grin.

"Oh, Bobby!" shouted Maritza, as he passed her the bouquet. "Thank you for everything! I loved the verses of poetry, and all of the clues. And thank you for these beautiful flowers."

"It was my pleasure," said Bobby. "Why don't we grab some lunch while we're here."

Hand in hand they set off and began their collegiate love story.

It had been two weeks since Mario had cooked with his pint-sized chefs. He was anxious to get back to them.

On the menu today was green salad and lasagna, which he had assembled beforehand. He would simply discuss the different layers with his students.

He was surprised when Emma Russo was the first student to arrive, and not little Joni.

"Mr. Mario, what is Italian seasoning? My grandmother uses it on practically *everything* she cooks," she inquired.

"Well, Emma, it is a combination of herbs such as basil, oregano, rosemary, thyme and garlic powder. I use it for several dishes that I make, such as lasagna, which I prepared for today," said Mario.

"Oh, I get it. Grandma uses it in her spaghetti sauce and even in her minestrone soup," said Emma.

"It would be great in those dishes," said Mario. "It just enhances the flavor of any recipe."

When the majority of the students had arrived, there was still no sign of Joni.

"Hello, my little chefs," welcomed Mario. "Let's begin by washing up."

When they were seated at kitchen tables, Mario addressed the crowd.

"Students, it seems that Joni is missing today. Does anyone know if she is sick?"

"Mr. Mario," offered Emma. "I think Joni moved away. We haven't seen her the past few weeks."

Mario was crushed. Now it was two women in his life who had slipped away—Miss Anonymous and Joni. He couldn't wait to finish his class and search out the director of the Boys and Girls Club, Vic Chambers.

He found Vic in his office where samples of sports equipment were scattered on his desk.

"Mario, I want to thank you again for the donations from a Taste of Oakview. These are samples from Oakview Sporting Goods. We will be using some of the money on sports equipment," said Vic.

"I am so glad to help out," said Mario. "This is a great place for kids, kind of a safe haven for them. I wanted to ask you about one of them, Joni Kim. The kids said that she has been absent for the past few weeks."

"Yes, what an unfortunate story. Her mother is in jail and will be for a very long time. She was running a brothel, and was sentenced to 20 years in prison after her trial. Joni has been living with her grandmother, who recently had a stroke and cannot take care of her. Joni has been put into a foster home," said Vic, a pained look on his face.

Mario was stunned and silent. He quickly gathered his thoughts.

"Vic, do you know where she is?"

"Sorry, Mario, I haven't a clue. Maybe Mayor Max could help you out. He is so knowledgeable about so many things," said Vic.

"Great idea," said Mario. "Thanks, Vic."

He just had to find his precious China doll.

Chapter Eight

September was in full swing as students returned to their classrooms and the weather had pivoted, producing a welcomed chill in the air.

With all of the plans drawn up with her architect, and a construction crew on deck, Sandy was ready to break ground on the new Sandy's Dandies. A small crowd—including Mario, Buddy, Mayor Max and Harley—were witness to this new start for Sandy, who was anxious to return to her former life as a bakery owner. She had enjoyed making treats at the Pizza Project, but it was time to move on.

Mayor Max welcomed the crowd in his usual affable manner.

"Welcome everyone! What a great day for Sandy, and for all of Oakview! Sandy, you have endured quite a loss, but the hope is for a return to a new and improved Sandy's Dandies. We will all be on hand the first of the year for your grand opening. Congratulations, Sandy, on this new beginning!"

The crowd applauded as Sandy ceremoniously dug a shovel of dirt and the groundbreaking was complete. Buddy passed around glazed donuts and cups of coffee to the bystanders.

Mario took Max aside and inquired about an office visit.

"Mario, you can come by between 10 and 11 this morning. I have a very light schedule today. Don't forget I'm located at the bank."

"Thanks a lot, Max. I'll be there."

Max had temporarily moved the offices of Maxwell Dunlap and Associates to the Oakview First Bank, as the offices were undergoing a remodeling to include a playroom for little EJ, who was currently in a baby swing and being watched by his birth mother, Lexi Cassidy. It seems that Lexi had a part-time job as a receptionist for Mayor Max.

She welcomed Mario and informed Max that he was there.

"Wow, this little guy is sure growing," said Mario, nodding to the flaxen-haired toddler.

"He sure is! He is 16 months old now!" said Lexi, bragging like any other mom would. This new job was a godsend for her, as she got to see more of EJ on a regular basis.

"Mario, come in," said Max, giving a brief wave to his son, who responded with sweet baby cooing and smiling, showing off his four teeth.

Once he was seated, Mario broached the subject of his visit.

"Max, I have been teaching cooking classes at the Boys and Girls Club for the past few months, and I have become quite fond of one of my students, Joni Kim. Vic Chambers told me that Joni's mother is in prison and her grandmother, her guardian, recently fell ill and cannot care for Joni anymore. Unfortunately, Joni is now in the foster care system. I was wondering if you could help me find her."

Mario was hopeful that Max had the answers he was searching for.

"Well, Mario, I will start with court records to find out any information that I can on her mother. And I will inquire at Child Protective Services to see if they have any information on Joni's whereabouts. A child enters the foster care system after a report is filed with CPS. Reasons for moving a child into foster care usually include neglect, abuse, or abandonment by a child's parents or guardians."

He added, "Give me a week, and I will see what I can find."

The relief on Mario's face said it all.

"Max, I am really grateful. I will make an appointment with Lexi on my way out."

The men shook hands, and Mario made the appointment, saying a prayer of gratitude and hope.

The Misfits assembled that afternoon, and David gave an update on his college classes, a martini in his hand.

"Davey, do you miss Notre Dame," asked Buddy, who was off for the day but chose to stay for the camaraderie and to keep Sandy company. He had really come to love the Misfits and reveled in these impromptu chats.

"Well, Buddy, I don't miss the snow! I do miss the environment, however. The architecture is truly magnificent and the brick edifices are a sight to behold."

He added, "I am glad that I chose to set down new roots in Oakview, especially since I get to be in the presence of my darling daughter."

As if on cue, Cassie entered the Pizza Project.

"Hey, Dad! Hey, Buddy!" She grabbed a quick hug from David before handing over a calendar from Bennington High School.

Buddy and Sandy took their leave, anxious to be alone in the man cave.

"So, here is a printout of our calendar. As you can see, Poetry Comes Alive is in mid-October. You will be judging the finals of the competition, on October 16," Cassie opened up to October and pointed out the dates.

"Excellent! It is a Thursday, when I have no college classes. But I am sure my students would welcome a day off if I were teaching that day!" David said.

"Not this student," replied Maritza, eavesdropping as she bussed tables. "I love your class! I am just unsure of what Shakespeare says about the marriage of true minds in 'Sonnet 116,' which we are reading for tomorrow."

David laughed, and Cassie offered her thoughts.

"I think Shakespeare is trying to define love by telling what it is and what it's not," she said. "'The marriage of true minds' is perfect and unchanging. True love is an enduring, unbending commitment between people and a bond so powerful that only death can reshape it."

"Bravo, my clever Cassie!" David clapped. "I'll bet you were a straight-A student!"

Cassie blushed, and admitted, "Pretty much!"

"Thanks, Cassie, for being my personal Cliffs Notes!" Maritza said, wiping down a table.

Just then, a soccer team entered the restaurant, ending the mid-afternoon chatter.

Mario braced himself for the onslaught and remembered that Steve was bringing his soon-to-be stepson and teammates for an after-practice kick-off party to begin their season.

"Welcome, Thundercats!" he called out and mused for the umpteenth time at how silly soccer team names are. He had heard them all, from Avengers to Blazers to Goal Diggers, the worst of them all.

Steve and his assistant coaches grabbed some beers— which Steve poured—as the team began its assault on the arcade machines.

Mario snagged a chance for a quick conversation with his best friend.

"I can't believe how tall Jacob is," said Mario, pointing out Emi's son, a mop of blond hair atop his head.

"He's eating us out of house and home! I never thought a six-year-old would have such a huge appetite," said Steve, marveling at all of the things he had learned about kids since Emi, Jacob, and her daughter Beth had come into his life. Beth was ten, and already a mini fashionista.

"How are the wedding preparations?" Mario inquired, and cringed when he remembered that he still didn't have a plus one. And the wedding was three months away!

"Pretty much everything is finished," said Steve. "Emi has done a great job planning the wedding. She has cut back her hours at Mayor Max's so she can concentrate on everything that needs to be done."

"I was at Max's office the other day, and Lexi was working. I think it's great that she can be around EJ more often."

"Yes, that sure worked out," said Mario.

The pizza was ready, and Maritza placed it on two tables with pitchers of root beer, plates, and napkins. Within minutes, the pans were empty, as the Thundercats devoured the pies.

Mario was glad when the team's 90 minutes were up and promised Steve that he would come by the pub soon.

Gloria was enjoying a quiet afternoon with her companions, a cup of tea and a romance novel, when David returned to the inn. He was dressed in a suit, his usual attire for the classroom.

"A gracious good day, Gloria. How are you doing this fine afternoon?" he asked.

Instead of being miffed that her silence was broken, Gloria welcomed David into her sacred space. The two had been spending more time together when he wasn't discussing Shakespeare or teaching writing, and she wasn't doing her daily chores.

"Just enjoying my novel," she lifted her book to show him, suddenly a bit embarrassed that it wasn't a higher form of literature.

"To each his own when it comes to literature," said David. "Although I must admit that I have never read a romance novel, which I assume is the genre of the book that you are reading."

"Yes, it is," she admitted.

"Describe the premise." David was curious to know about the plot.

"Well, the novel centers around a nurse in a hospital's emergency ward. She ends up falling in love with one of her patients whom she nurses back to life after a near-death experience in a car accident," said Gloria.

"Sounds scintillating!!" declared David. "Maybe I will borrow it when you're finished with it, and we can have a literary powwow!"

Gloria laughed and thought how nice it was to be in the company of someone so intelligent but with a down-to-earth nature.

"Let's do it!" she said, a broad grin on her pretty face.

Debra had to admit that she was a bit jealous of her son, thriving in his relationship with Maritza. She wished that she had someone in her life. It seemed the only men in her life were Bobby and John Ramsey, her chef. John was in a relationship with Ronny Goldwyn, one of the assistant principals under Cassie's leadership at Bennington. This was his first year at the school.

She knew that she often drove John crazy, especially with the changes that she had been dying to make, but he was very patient with her. Lately, they had been confiding in each another.

"John, tell me about your relationship with Ronny," Debra wanted to know more about her head chef other than the ingredients of his pesto sauce.

"It's going really well, Debra. As a matter of fact, I am planning to propose soon! I visited with his parents on the sly last week when he was at a soccer game and asked for their permission. They were so thrilled!"

"Oh John, that's wonderful! Do you have a ring? And where will you propose?"

"Yup, I purchased two bands for us to wear during our engagement and beyond. When I went to the jeweler's I surreptitiously brought in Ronny's high school ring. Again, that was done when Ronny was busy at a school function— this time, it was a play. The proposal destination is a secret!"

John beamed in spilling the deets, pleased with himself and with all that he had accomplished.

"John, Ronny is a gem, as are you. I like it when he comes and visits, but I question his penchant for pineapple and Canadian bacon pizza. That is about the only kind that I won't eat—or maybe anchovies, too!"

Debra felt good letting out a belly laugh, something she rarely does these days. She made a note to herself to do that more often.

The best medicine, as they say.

A week after his initial appointment with Max, Mario returned to the bank for his follow-up visit. He was pleased to see Emi at the receptionist's desk.

"Mario!" Emi jumped up to hug her fiancé's best friend.

"So good to see you, Emi! I hear that you are quite the wedding planner! Steve keeps bragging about how things are going well with your deft hand."

Emi blushed.

"Well, I feel pretty good about how things are coming along. You know, Mario, that we haven't gotten your reply card in the mail. We know you're coming, but I have no idea who your plus one will be," said Emi, a questioning look upon her face.

"Well, that makes two of us!" bellowed Mario. "I am waiting to see if a miracle happens before I submit it. "

"You never know what might happen in the next three months," assured Emi.

"Yeah, you never know," said Mario, trying to convince himself.

"I wondered what all of the tomfoolery was," said Max, who emerged from his office with little EJ in tow, and passed him off to Emi.

"Come on back, Mario."

When they were in the enclosed office, Mario nervously awaited Max's findings. And he worried about Joni every day, all day.

"I know you are anxious to learn about Joni, so I will cut to the chase," said Max.

"For starters, her mother Barbara is in a women's prison in Central California. She has done 3 years out of a possible 20, and so far has been a model inmate. She got caught running a brothel, as you know."

He continued, "Child Protective Services received word from her uncle, who lives in Arizona, and papers were processed from there. Don't know why the uncle isn't taking care of Joni, but I did find out that he has five children and works two jobs, as an architect and college professor. I think we can put two and two together on that one."

"Joni is living in Glendale, about 20 minutes from here. She is staying with George and Penelope Collins, a childless couple who cannot have children. He is a doctor and she is a fourth-grade teacher."

"Wow, Max! You sure found out a lot in just a week. Do you think that this Collins couple will want to adopt Joni?"

"I haven't a clue."

Across town, in the basement of the Oakview Baptist Church, Laney sat apprehensively in a folding chair, her hand linked with Scott's as she summoned her courage to speak.

She stood and made her declaration, still holding John's hand.

"I am Laney, and I'm an alcoholic."

"Hi Laney," came the collaborative response from those gathered for an Alcoholics Anonymous meeting. This was her first meeting, after much soul-searching and deep discussions with Scott, who attended his own Gamblers Anonymous meetings in the very same basement.

Despite her jitters, she was glad that she came.

Her new journey was just beginning.

Chapter Nine

"Misfits, assemble!" demanded Buddy as he barged through the door of the Project. He had just been visiting Sandy at PP #2, where she had been making desserts for a banquet that evening.

"I have a huge announcement! The hugest!" His arms spread wide at the pronouncement.

All eyes were riveted on him as he was ready to burst. He turned sharply in Mario's direction.

"Bitch with a Bun is your Karaoke Angel!"

Suddenly, everyone was talking at once. How could it be? They are two very distinct people. Heck, Debra probably hasn't worn makeup a day in her life.

Questions, questions, questions.

"Buddy, may I ask how you came to this ridiculous conclusion?" fumed Mario. "Have you been smoking something funny?"

"Nah, I haven't smoked pot since before the Navy. Anyway, Sandy has been spending the past few days at PP #2, as you know. She informs me that Debra sings all the time, and she recognized a few of her songs from Kickin' Karaoke. She swears it's the same beautiful voice."

"Has John said anything about this?" Mario asked Buddy.

"John doesn't go to Kickin' Karaoke. He says it's a busman's holiday," Buddy replied. "He doesn't know about your angel."

Mario was beside himself, and he was suddenly mad at Debra. How could she do this to him? But what did she do? She shared her wonderful talent with the Oakview community, that's what she did. And made him lie awake many, many nights, thinking, dreaming, thinking, dreaming.

He knew she was working for the night manager that evening, and he decided to drop by after his Project closed.

He had to get to the bottom of this stupid conundrum.

The lone person in PP #2, Debra was wiping down tables when Mario charged through the front door.

"Are you my Karaoke Angel?" he shouted, his voice raised and his thoughts a jumbled mess.

"Excuse me?" Debra answered. "Your what?"

"I mean, are you the person who sang so beautifully all summer and just left without even letting us know your name?"

"Yes, I am. Let me explain," she said, going back into the kitchen to deposit her towels.

She faced Mario and fessed up.

"Singing is my passion. I just wanted to get up on stage, sing my songs, then leave. I didn't want people to know who I was because I wanted to establish myself in this job first and gain some credibility. I hope that you can understand."

She looked half terrified and felt half guilty.

"I cannot believe this!" Mario howled. "I spent so much time wondering who you were, when you were right here all along. You are someone I don't know and someone I don't especially care for."

"I am sorry, Mario."

All of a sudden, Mario snapped. Something inexplicable overcame him, and he couldn't stop. He was almost frightened of himself.

He grabbed Debra and placed her up against the massive stainless steel refrigerator. And started to kiss her.

"You bitch! You beautiful, wonderful, delectable bitch!"

Yeah, he was temporarily insane—that was for sure.

He kept kissing her.

Somehow, Debra was no longer scared. She grabbed Mario around the waist and clung on to him, matching him kiss for kiss. It had been a long time since she was caught in a man's embrace, other than her philandering ex-husband.

As if both were hungry for each other, they started to touch and explore, hastily and without stopping.

Wordlessly, Mario moved Debra to the break room, where they continued kissing and touching on the couch.

Mario was stunned at his behavior, which was totally unprecedented.

He stopped kissing Debra and tried to find the words.

"I am sorry for calling you a bitch," he said. "My thoughts are muddled and confused. You don't know how much sleep I lost because of you, wondering who you were, grasping for any information about you, even your name. I called you my Karaoke Angel. That is the name I created for you because you looked like an angel with the lights falling across your beautiful hair, which your bun disguises."

"My bun is part of my business persona," said Debra, "along with these glasses and the boxy uniforms. I am very serious when it comes to my profession."

"Well, at this moment, I don't care about your business persona," said Mario as he ran his hand down her arm. "I care about your *feminine* persona."

And he returned to kissing Debra.

A few days later, Buddy was all set for This Day in History as he came through the door, a bit more restrained this time.

"Hey, boss! Guess what happened on this day in history?"

"What happened, Buddy?"

"On October 1, 1908, the first Model T Ford rolled off the assembly line. It was hailed as 'the car of the century'."

Wait for it...

"What was the first car Henry Fordasaurus invented? A Model T-Rex!"

A while later, Buddy's curiosity got the better of him.

"So, Boss, do you think it's true that Debra is your Karaoke Angel? Sandy swears it's true."

"Well, I don't have time for riddles and speculation," said Mario. "If that's the same person, she has a beautiful voice. Let's leave it at that."

Mario was cleverly dipping into Buddy's playbook about kissing and telling.

That afternoon, David came to the Project with Gloria Sheffield, of all people. Talk about speculation!

Mario suspected that today's Scrabble game was a no-go. Too bad! He wanted to keep his reign at the top of the leaderboard.

"Everyone, this is Gloria Sheffield, in case you have not had the pleasure of meeting the proprietor of the Hope Inn. Gloria, we are the Misfits. And Sandy back in the kitchen is what you might call Misfit-adjacent." Sandy waved to the two.

"My dear Gloria, what would you like to drink this afternoon? I usually imbibe a dry martini," David offered.

"Chardonnay, please," said Gloria, though she was not much of a drinker.

After David brought their drinks, Buddy had to ask.

"The usual?"

"Well, Buddy my good man, I would say no to the usual and see what the lady would like."

David and Gloria had decided on a pepperoni pizza and salad.

"What is the usual for you?" Gloria was curious.

"Microwave popped corn!"

Gloria let out a huge laugh. He's down-to-earth, all right.

Porter and Bobby were on a double date with Sophia and Maritza, one of their many. The fall had brought many changes to the busy four, with Bobby enjoying his initial collegiate football experience, Maritza loving her English class and watching Bobby's games, Sophia working hard on ASB duties, and Porter piling up college recruitment letters.

Porter had one last college visit, which he didn't get around to in the summer. The next weekend, he would be traveling to the University of San Diego, a short plane flight from Oakview.

"Hey, Maritza, how do you like Dr. Cummings's class?" asked Porter, as he dug into a plate of spaghetti. The couples were dining at Primavera, a rival of PP #1 and PP #2.

"You guys, he is the greatest professor! I love his sense of humor, and his knowledge of Shakespeare is through the roof!" she exclaimed as she tore off a piece of roll and dipped it in butter.

"Well, I think he likes my mom," Porter declared. "They seem to be spending a lot of time together lately."

"Wow!" said Bobby. "I guess old people can use some companionship, too. Do you think they're doing it?"

"Bobby! Respect your elders!" said Sophia, who had a bit of a bossy streak in her, much to the chagrin of her twin brother, Mark. "Besides, I think it's great that they found each other. They probably have a lot of stories to tell one another."

The foursome decided to go miniature golfing after leaving Primavera, though the October chill was nibbling at their cheeks.

All the more reason to cuddle with your significant other.

Mario spent Monday morning in contemplation about what have come to be the two most important women in his life: a 40-something restaurant manager and an 11-year-old girl.

What to do about these ladies?

He and Debra had their little make-out session in PP #2, but seemed to have been avoiding each other since, perhaps each feeling awkward with the come-from-nowhere lip lock.

Meanwhile, he snagged the email address of George Collins after doing a bit of sleuthing and decided to send him a message. Maybe Mario could come for a visit with Joni. But how do you start an email like that?

His musings came to a halt as he prepared minestrone soup for his little chefs, who would put all of the ingredients together that afternoon. Mario would also give a short lesson on making garlic bread.

Just as he was putting out the aprons for his mini cooks, who walked in but little Joni, accompanied by a woman whom he thought must be Penelope Collins.

His heart skipped a beat as he spied his little China doll, adorable in denim coveralls.

The woman introduced herself, and said, "Mr. Bertolli, Joni talks about you all the time. I just had to bring her in and meet you." She shook his hand after Joni gave him a leg hug.

"I am so glad to see you, Joni! The little chefs and I have missed you so much! How are you?" asked Mario.

"Mr. Mario, my grandmother got really sick, and I have been staying with Mr. and Mrs. Collins. They are very nice to me, but we don't cook much. I have missed all of you, too," said Joni as she again wrapped her arms around Mario's leg.

His heart was melting again. The power of an 11-year-old's affection.

Penelope remained for the lesson, and as the students were packing up, Mario grabbed her for a quick chat.

"Do you think that you are going to adopt Joni?" He needed an answer, pronto.

"Oh, heavens, no," said Penelope. "We are foster parents who temporarily care for children with the greatest needs. Child Protective Services calls upon us several times a year to help out. Because we are financially capable, we bring in children to help them get through tough times, until they are adopted."

"You are such generous people," said Mario. "Joni is lucky to have you."

"Thank you, Mario, for all that you have done for her. She simply adores you."

There went Mario's heart again. Tap, tap, tapping at his soul.

With Porter gone to San Diego for his final recruiting trip, Gloria decided to cook dinner for David on Saturday night. They were the only ones in the inn, as Debra and Bobby had decided to spend an impromptu weekend in Los Angeles, where Bobby had a football game at UCLA on Friday night. They would spend the rest of the weekend taking in

the sights, such as Hollywood Boulevard, the farmers'
market, and Venice Beach.

On Friday, Gloria printed out a formal dinner invitation
and taped it to David's door.

*Gloria Sheffield requests the honor of your presence at
dinner in the formal dining room of Hope Inn on Saturday,
October 5, at 6:00 sharp. Dress is semi-formal.*

*Drinks will be followed by a dinner of potato-crusted
salmon, asparagus with bacon and balsamic vinaigrette, and
parmesan risotto.*

*Dessert will include chocolate soufflé, shortbread
cookies, and, as an aperitif, Frangelico.*

Not too bad, Gloria thought to herself. Perhaps a way
to a man's heart *is* through his stomach.

David smiled as he read the invitation and thoughtfully
considered a gift that was worthy of his beautiful hostess.

He decided to take a lesson from Bobby's literary bent
and offer her a gift of poetry—his own book, written when he
was fresh out of graduate school, and navigating the
collegiate landscape as a newly minted English professor.

Only five copies of the book existed—three in David's
possession; one with Constance Daniels, with whom he had
broken up, but still remained close at publication time; and
one in the library at Notre Dame. Students liked to check it
out and snicker at their professor's verses, which really

proved to be quite good, as they discovered. That copy was weathered and weary, but it stood the test of time.

Saturday began bright for Gloria, as she gathered ingredients for dinner at the local market. Singing as she worked, she prepped as much as she could and wrote out a timeline for all of the dishes.

The soufflé would require the most attention: According to Martha Stewart, whose recipe Gloria was utilizing, prep time is 30 minutes and cooking time 50 minutes.

She would have to do some orchestration before dinner, cooking it as they sat down for the meal.

David was prompt...and very dapper. Gloria was used to seeing him in a suit, but now he was in khaki pants and a long-sleeved Oxford shirt, the sleeves rolled up halfway. He kissed her hand and passed her a gift bag.

"Oh, David! How wonderful! Your own book of poetry! I will cherish it always!" Gloria wanted to dig right in and begin reading, but that would have to wait. She had a soufflé to consider!

Though they came from different worlds, Gloria and David experienced a confluence of the two, as they shared more and more of their lives.

David had already known about Gloria's former husband, and Gloria was aware of David's former relationship with Constance Daniels. But what mattered most to them were their children, especially since each of them had only one child on whom they each doted.

Over dinner, Gloria shared that she was not looking forward to the inevitable empty nest that she would be facing next summer. But she was so happy that Porter had so many schools from which to choose, all of them with partial or full scholarships.

David mentioned that his landing at Oakview gave him a new lease on life. Although he was aware of Cassie's triumphs and tragedies, thanks to Constance, he felt blessed to meet her in person and to become a part of her life. He told Gloria his biggest and dearest dream: to become a grandfather. That would be the icing on the cake, or, to David, the chocolate ganache on top of a salted caramel tart. He was a dessert connoisseur.

And he loved the soufflé, which he savored with the rich hazelnut liqueur.

"My dear Gloria, you have certainly outdone yourself this evening!" he declared. "I was aware of your skillful prowess in the kitchen when it came to our delightful breakfasts, but I had no idea that your culinary skills extended to such lavish and wonderful dishes. I am most grateful for the excellent dinner and the beautiful company."

"David, I have so enjoyed our evening. Why don't we go out back and watch the stars and sit in the pool lounges? I have a huge blanket we can use, and we can light the fire pit," she suggested.

"Excellent idea! I will see if I can point out some constellations if it is clear enough."

And so, they shared a blanket and sat side by side by the crackling fire, relishing in this newfound relationship which bridged the gap between their worlds.

Chapter Ten

"Mario, are you sure of this?" asked Mayor Max for the fifth time. "You are a super busy guy with not one, but two restaurants to run, and you only have one day off a week."

"Max, I'm serious. I want to adopt Joni and give her a forever home. I can always buy a larger house and cut back on my work hours. And I have my siblings who are willing to help out with babysitting. Does an 11-year-old even need babysitting?"

"I have no clue. My kid is only 17 months old. For your frame of reference, we have two part-time nannies, plus when EJ is in the office, we have Emi and Lexi to help out. It really does take a village when it comes to child care."

"Thanks for the info, Max. Please let me know what steps I need to adopt a child. I know that the Collinses have no desire to adopt Joni, and no one seems to have stepped up to do so. Please let me know if anyone does."

"Will do, Mario. I will be in touch when I have some answers, and I will share my experiences with you."

"Thanks, Max. I really appreciate it."

One problem down, one to go.

Mario decided to break the ice with Debra, whom he had not seen for 10 days, much too long to not see his Karaoke Angel, in the guise of a prim and proper restaurateur.

He remained in a perplexed state.

Since she was finished with her shift at 4:00, he ambled by at 3:30 and caught her in the midst of a very crowded PP #2, with a Little League team of girls scattered all over the place.

Grabbing an apron, he decided to chip in and ended up staying an hour after calling his own Project to inform Maritza.

"Mario, you were like someone sent from above," said Debra after the team had departed. "I don't know what I would have done without you. I had a server call in sick today."

"Well, that panicked look on your face when I first came in said it all," said Mario, discarding his apron and poised to return to his own restaurant.

He decided to bite the bullet.

"Debra, would you like to go out on Sunday night? We both have no work on Mondays, so we can stay out late."

"Sure, Mario. Sure. What did you have in mind?"

"I thought we might try Maison Francois. Have you ever been there?"

"No, never."

"They have a dress code. Shirts and ties for the men, dressy pants or dresses for the ladies. It is a top-notch restaurant."

"Sounds great!"

"Okay, I will pick you up at the inn at 6:30."

Debra didn't remember the last time she donned a dress, except for her Kickin' Karaoke performances. For her first date with Mario, she decided to wear the form-fitting black number that she wore her first time on the stage. She curled her hair in the cascades that he had grown to love, and brought a bright-red wrap for this chilly mid-October evening.

He was stunned when he knocked on her door at the inn. Memories of seeing her backlit on the stage returned to him as he uttered, "You are stunning, Debra. Just stunning."

She was taken aback at the compliment and whispered her reply in a word: "Thanks."

Maison Francois was a beautiful, intimate restaurant with tables bathed in candlelight and soft instrumental music from a guitarist serving as a soothing backdrop. The effect was pure romance and the menu magnifique.

Debra ordered chicken cordon bleu, and Mario chose beef bourguignon, the specialty of the house. She had the Pinot Grigio, and he picked a nice Pinot Noir.

The dinner was superb, as was the company. Their conversation covered multiple topics, from Bobby and Maritza's relationship to Mario's cooking classes with his little chefs. He didn't want to disclose his desire to adopt Joni, as there were still so many unanswered questions.

When Mario walked Debra to her room, she thanked him for the lovely evening and asked if he wanted to come in.

"Where is Bobby?" he inquired.

"He is staying with Porter tonight. I think that Gloria is bringing them to the batting cages and then to dinner."

"Okay," he said, feeling like a 16-year-old about to have sex for the first time.

Mario and Debra reprised their groping session from PP #2 immediately upon jumping onto Debra's bed. They were still hungry, still passionate, still longing for a touch, a taste, a kiss. And things went to a whole new level.

Second problem, solved.

The Misfits gathered a few days later, and David explained the rules of Poetry Comes Alive.

"So, my friends. I am going to be judging this contest tomorrow that involves students reciting and performing poems. They are judged on their poise, accuracy, performance, and physical presence. My darling Cassie is seeking the first-place position in the county for one of her students, which apparently has gone to Bristol Academy for the past several years."

"Davey, do you have to know all of the poems beforehand?" asked Buddy.

"No, there is a separate accuracy judge who offers a score for the precise word-for-word recitation. I will be focusing mostly on presentation and the execution of the poems."

"Come back tomorrow and let us know how it went," requested Buddy.

"Oh, you can bet on that!" promised David.

David was judging the final round of PCA; the winner of this round would be advancing to the county contest, and the winner of the county would be traveling to Sacramento for the California state finals.

He was excited to come onto the campus of Bennington High School for the first time, to see where his daughter spent her days as principal.

In the gym, he took his place and was handed seven tally sheets for the seven performers.

Most students did an excellent job of executing their poetry, a few stumbled and mumbled, and one just said he was sorry and exited the gym.

All of the judges submitted their tally sheets, and the ultimate winner was Jenny Cooper, who performed E.E.

Cummings's [i carry your heart with me (i carry it in], a favorite of Bobby's.

"Dad! Do you want to join me and Jenny in the county finals next week?" Cassie asked as she hugged her father.

"I would love to! Where do we go for that contest?"

"The county Department of Education," she said. "It is at 6:30 next Thursday evening. Maybe we can grab some dinner beforehand."

"Sounds fabulous!"

Sandy was feeling outstanding about the progress of the new and improved Sandy's Dandies. Each day as she and Buddy left work mid-afternoon, they would happen by the construction, now in its third month. She had continued the motif of the flowered booths and tablecloths and curtains, and added a second stove and second dishwasher, as well as 100 extra square feet, expanding her dining area.

A few times a week, they went back to her cottage to pick up mail and to make sure that everything was okay, but she continued to stay at the man cave.

She had no desire to leave it...and Buddy.

Buddy was due for some vacation time, and that evening after dinner, they chatted about the possibilities over coffee and oatmeal raisin cookies, made by Sandy, of course.

"Darlin,' where do you want to go for our vacation? We have five whole days to ourselves."

"Gosh, Buddy, I have no idea. But I feel okay leaving the construction site because things are going so well over there."

"Okay, let's think about it the next few days."

Ultimately, they chose Las Vegas and booked flights for the next week.

Maisie had been sneaking food to the homeless man— whose name turned out to be Bill Hamilton—on a daily basis before he set out to whatever destination he chose for the day.

A week went by and she didn't see him on her doorstep, and she began to worry about him.

Had he passed away somehow? Perhaps attacked by a coyote or another homeless person?

Another two weeks transpired, and one day a handsome young man appeared at her door. She just figured that he needed to have his suits dry cleaned, but he didn't have any suits in hand.

"Maisie, it's Bill. I know you don't recognize me with my beard shaven and wearing some decent clothes."

Maisie was stunned and just stared at Bill, astounded at the transformation. He was really a good-looking man under all of that bushy beard and filthy clothes.

"How did you manage to undergo such a change?" she asked, marveling at the miraculous before and after.

"To be truthful, I got tired roaming the streets. If you can believe it, I am a college graduate who just fell on hard times and ended up homeless. I heard about the opening of a new men's shelter in Glendale, and I began living there. The good people who run it offer job interviews and have clothing that has been donated. I ended up interviewing for a job as a bank teller at Oakview First Bank, which I got. I will be at the shelter until I can afford to live in an apartment."

He continued, "I want to tell you how much your offerings of food have meant to me these past few months. You gave me hope to improve my life and faith in people again. I just want to say thank you."

Maisie began to cry and reached for a hug from the person she used to shoo away like an unwanted animal. And her faith was restored as well.

Mario had an appointment with Max to discuss adoption procedures. He was worried that somehow the Collinses would change their minds and want to adopt Joni. After all, she was an adorable child with the biggest heart.

The past few weeks, Max had been gathering information for Mario, and he was ready for a full report.

"Good to see you, Mario," Max said as he shook his hand and led him into his office. "I've got lots to share with you."

"I am so glad to know it, Max," said Mario. "Lay it on me."

"Okay, the first step is to partner with an adoption agency that can help mediate the process and create an adoption plan for you. It will be a true partnership—you and the adoption agency. Take it from one who knows. Harley and I went through this same process in adopting EJ."

He continued, "There are private and public adoption agencies. Each county has its own department of social services responsible for caring for children in foster care. That is the public agency. A private adoption agency is licensed and regulated by the state the parties reside in. This can be a more expensive platform, but the quality of care is solid and perhaps a better choice."

"Will the agency check me out thoroughly? And perhaps interview my friends and associates?" asked Mario.

"Yes, you will have to fill out an in-depth questionnaire. It is important to be 100% honest in your responses. And they will make appointments for interviews with those who know you best. The agency Harley and I chose did the same thing."

Max continued, "Ultimately, Joni's uncle will be the person to sign the papers if the adoption goes through. He has power of attorney as a representative of the Kim family, as Joni's mother wants nothing to do with her, sadly. Talk about abandonment. I learned this through my conversations with the uncle."

Mario exited Max's office with more questions than he entered with. But the hassle, headaches, and paperwork will all be worth it when he has the privilege of being called Dad.

Chapter Eleven

Like two kids let loose on a week-long vacation from school, Buddy and Sandy made Las Vegas their personal playground.

The bright lights beckoned them to enjoy the sights and sounds—the glorious fountains of the Bellagio, the massive Ferris wheel at the Linq Hotel, shopping at Caesar's Palace, just to name a few.

And the food was incredible, their few extra pounds a testament to that fact at week's end.

"Oh, Buddy! I am having the time of my life! As you know, this is my first time visiting Las Vegas, and I think it is absolutely fascinating!" Sandy gushed as they took a tram to the MGM Grand, their destination for five nights.

"Darlin', you deserve a great vacation. I hope that you will consider a spa day while we're here. I saw on a brochure that the spa overlooks the pool. That's really cool!" Buddy encouraged a day of pampering for his sweetheart.

Buddy devised a plan. He had been contemplating this vacation for weeks, and had purchased a one-carat diamond engagement ring at Glendale Jewelers so that he might propose to Sandy wherever they landed.

He would do it at the top of the High Roller, the 550-foot-tall Ferris wheel on the premises of the Linq Hotel. Touted as the world's tallest, it is a slow-moving attraction that takes 30 minutes to complete. Plenty of time for a proposal.

The next day, Buddy and Sandy boarded the High Roller, and the bartender in their cabin approached them, offering a bucket with champagne and two glasses. Buddy had everything pre-arranged.

Sandy was shocked. She just thought it was a very nice gesture on Buddy's part as they slowly began their ascent.

When they were nearing the top, the bartender phoned the ride operator, who paused the pod briefly so that Buddy had time for his moves.

Dropping to one knee, Buddy produced a ring box and opened it so that Sandy might view the sparkly magnificence of the engagement ring.

"Sandy, you are my lady love, my best friend, my confidante. I love you so much and I want to spend the rest of my life loving you and caring for you. Will you marry me?"

"Oh, Buddy! Yes! Yes! Yes!" Sandy threw her arms around him as he stood, and the audience in their cabin exploded into spontaneous applause.

"Our lives together have just begun," whispered Buddy as he kissed his fiancée gently on the lips.

In the aftermath of their lovemaking, Mario and Debra lay entwined, their labored breathing creating a rhythmic cadence as they clung to each other. He stroked her beautiful hair as she indulged in Mario's touch, so soft and gentle.

Like the angel that she was to Mario, Debra began singing the Beatles' "In My Life." Mario reveled in the beauty of that lovely voice, singing just for him. He closed his eyes and took it all in.

It was a precious Monday morning in Mario's loft, the Project quiet and the place their private oasis.

"I need to tell you something that only Max knows," Mario said. "I feel the need to be totally transparent with you."

"What is it, Mario?" Debra was afraid that he might say that he was married or in another relationship, foolish thoughts that she quickly abandoned.

"I am in the process of adopting an 11-year-old little girl whom I met in my cooking classes at the Boys and Girls Club. Her mother is in prison, and her grandmother, who is her guardian, recently had a stroke and cannot care for her."

"Wow, Mario! That is really something. But how will you be able to supervise your two businesses and take on all of the responsibilities of becoming a father?"

"I have siblings willing to help with babysitting, and I am going to cut back a bit on my hours at work. Tomorrow at our Chamber of Commerce meeting I will share this news with the group and see if they have any ideas."

"I wish you much luck with the adoption process. I heard that it can be grueling." Debra kissed him softly on the lips, and the aftermath suddenly shifted to foreplay once again. Plain and simple, they couldn't get enough of each other.

At the Chamber of Commerce meeting the next day, Mario waited until the end of the agenda to reveal his secret. Among the items discussed was Maisie's homeless friend; she took such pride in sharing Bill's success story.

"If there are no other items to address, I wanted to switch gears to a more personal topic. I am in the process of adopting an 11-year-old girl."

Everyone—except Max and Debra, bless them—spoke at once.

"Are you crazy?"

"How can you become a father with all of your responsibilities?"

"What will happen to your restaurants?"

"What do you know about caring for a child?"

It was quite the barrage. And one that Mario steeled himself for.

"Everyone, calm down, please," he requested, or rather, demanded.

Mario proceeded to tell the backstory of his relationship with Joni and all of the sordid pieces of the Kim family's life.

"Well, I think it is just wonderful!" offered Sabrina Patterson, herself the mother of two young boys. "Your life will be so enhanced by a child, Mario. You will wonder how you ever lived without her before the adoption."

"Sabrina, I really appreciate that. It means a lot to me."

Mario was near tears at that point. After a few more comments, he dismissed the Chamber and returned to his job, certain that he was doing the right thing.

As Buddy and Sandy were packing up for their return flight to Oakview, Buddy had a suggestion, as always.

"Darlin', you know that I always tend to be a man with a plan," he said, looking pretty proud at that statement, gazing at her with a twinkle in his eye.

She simply smiled and nodded. That was her man, always thinking.

"Well, I suggest that before we fly home, we get married! There are tons of wedding chapels within miles of here, and I'll bet it wouldn't take long. We have two hours until our flight. What do you say?"

"Oh, Buddy, will our friends ever forgive us for eloping? Don't you think that everyone would want to attend our wedding?" asked Sandy.

"Here I am with a plan again! How about if we get married this afternoon, and then hold the reception when your bakery is finished?"

"What a great idea!" Sandy flung her arms around Buddy's neck.

And then, they set out for the Chapel of the Flowers to become Mr. and Mrs. Rutherford Thomas. No wonder he went by Buddy!

The next day, Buddy burst into the Project for a late shift and secretly hid his wedding ring in his pocket. He had a CD in hand, much to the curiosity of the Misfits.

"Hello, Misfits!" he bellowed. "I have something to show you. Let's assemble!"

He went up to one of the many televisions in the room—one with a CD player still intact—and played the disc for the onlookers.

At the chapel, Sandy was resplendent in a beautiful white knee-length dress, and Buddy was dapper in a suit. Since they had just one hour to hunt for their wedding wardrobe, they did an excellent job.

A female officiant discussed the power of marriage, and the two-become-one miracle, and pronounced them husband and wife. Buddy kissed his bride.

A huge silence filled the room as everyone glanced at each other, wondering what to say, or do.

"Guys, I want you to be happy for us!" With that, Buddy produced his wedding ring and placed it on his left hand.

"We got engaged on top of the Linq Ferris wheel one day, and got married the next day. So, Mario, yesterday was a great day in history!"

At that, the Misfits broke into applause, and Buddy breathed a sigh of relief at the approval of these people who had come to play such an integral role in his life.

Gloria was making breakfast on a Tuesday, one of David's days off from Walker College, as his classes were only on Mondays and Wednesdays. He padded into the kitchen to see if he could assist the chief cook and bottle washer.

"Gloria, my lady! A very pleasant good morning to you! What is on the bill of fare this morning?"

"Hello, David. We have waffles with strawberries and/or blueberries and whipped cream, and Denver omelets with roasted potatoes. You can have any or all of the choices."

"I choose the omelet without the potatoes. Since I have been enjoying my stay at this wonderful inn, I am afraid that I have gained a few pounds. Perhaps I should be walking more, or maybe join the Oakview Gym."

"David, you are just fine the way you are!" assured Gloria. "Let me throw in a few potatoes."

David enjoyed the company of Gloria as he hopped onto a stool in her kitchen island. Suddenly, Porter came barging in, interrupting their conversation.

"Hello, Dr. Cummings," Porter said, a bit on the frosty side. He wasn't too sure about this liaison with his mother.

"Porter! Tell me how senior year is going. We haven't conversed in such a long time. Did you make your college choice?"

"Well, Dr. Cummings, the year is going well, and I think that I am going to choose the University of San Diego, which is only 90 minutes from Oakview. I was offered a full scholarship for baseball. That doesn't happen at every college or university. Some offer partial scholarships. And I will have a single room in the dorms."

"Porter, how wonderful!!! If you need help in any way, please let me know. What will be your major? Perhaps I can help you choose some classes."

"I am already registered for classes, but thanks for the offer."

Pivoting in a heartfelt manner, Porter had a thought.

"Dr. Cummings, would you accompany my mom and me when I go to USD for move-in weekend? It is months away, but I know that she will be very sad at having an empty nest."

"I would be delighted to join you and your mother, Porter! It is a beautiful university with a stellar reputation. You will be a Torero!"

Porter was slowly accepting the fact that his mother had a man in her life, a true novelty. Heck, she deserved it after putting up with an addict husband who abused her. Who knows? Maybe he can get some extra help when his English class reads *Hamlet* next month.

Couldn't hurt to ask.

Mario was glad to have a reprieve from the adoption process when he, Steve, and Steve's groomsmen gathered in Palm Springs for the bachelor party in November.

The weather was beautiful as they made their ascent in the Palm Springs Aerial Tramway—touted as the world's largest rotating tram car. The ride offers picturesque vistas of the valley floor below Mt. San Jacinto State Park, their destination.

Once at the top, they ate lunch at the Peaks Restaurant and had drinks at the Lookout Lounge afterward.

It was a truly spectacular sight to behold for the men, and Steve, the planner for this event, was glad that he had chosen it.

Since it was unseasonably warm, they spent the rest of the afternoon poolside before going to dinner.

After returning to their suite later that evening, they were all playing video games when there was a knock at the door.

Two strippers descended on the men, and Steve was in utter shock.

"Hey, guys, I didn't plan this part of the weekend!" he yelled out as the girls brought in a boom box and began dancing to the music.

"I did!" confessed Steve's brother Frank, raising his hand. "Have fun, bro!"

Mario certainly was going to omit this little adventure when he gave Debra a run-down on the bachelor party. Yes, indeed.

At the county finals for Poetry Comes Alive, Jenny Cooper took first place, and would be traveling to Sacramento for the state contest just after Thanksgiving. Marilyn James was taken aback that one of her Bristol Academy students didn't take the top prize, but she was gracious in congratulating Cassie.

When Jenny's name was called, Cassie jumped up and robustly hugged David.

"We did it, Dad! We did it!!!" Cassie exclaimed. "You have to come to Sacramento with Jenny, her parents, and me!"

"I wouldn't miss it for the world, my darling daughter!"

Cassie looked forward to having her father to herself. Perhaps the time might afford the opportunity for a long talk, so that she could glean answers to so many questions that had been percolating since the discovery of her birth parents.

Chapter Twelve

November was swiftly flying by as Oakview enjoyed the changing of the oak tree leaves to become auburn, scarlet, and copper, depending on the tree variety. Temperatures dropped, and the woodsy smell of chimney fires permeated the late-autumn air.

Thanksgiving was a grand celebration, as David deemed it. Gloria, Porter, David, Debra, Bobby and Mario gathered for the feast to which all contributed.

Gloria provided ham and turkey; Mario brought bread; Debra made apple and pumpkin pies; David supplied ready-made mashed potatoes, cranberries and dressing from an upscale grocery store in Glendale; and the boys set the table and helped clean up.

After David's prayer to begin the meal, Gloria asked everyone to share what they were thankful for this year.

Porter went first.

"I am thankful for this inn, and for my mother, who has made it a true home for us and a new beginning. I love you, Mom."

Gloria was brought to tears as she replied, "I love you too, son."

She addressed the group: "I, too, am thankful for this inn, and for all of us who have come to call it a home. I know that, perhaps, one day David and Debra and Bobby will move on, but I am grateful that we all got to know one another."

Touched by Gloria's declaration, Debra weighed in.

"I, too, am thankful for this charming inn that Gloria designed as a wonderful place of solace and refuge. It has allowed Bobby and me to heal and brought us the freedom to move on with life. For that, I am extremely grateful."

Mario's turn was next.

"I am thankful for all of you at this table, even though one of you is at the top of the Scrabble leaderboard at the moment!"

He turned to David, who just chuckled.

Mario continued. "I am thankful for new people in my life, and new opportunities. And, if everything works out, I will have a 12-year-old daughter seated next to me next Thanksgiving."

Everyone applauded, and many shed tears of joy.

Bobby stepped up to offer his thanks.

"I am grateful for all of you, for Maritza, and for Lions football. I am glad that I chose Walker College and decided to stay home to be near you, Mom."

Debra smiled at her son, proud of the fine young man he had become.

Finally, it was David's time to shine.

"In *Twelfth Night*, William Shakespeare's noble character Sebastian proclaims 'I can no other answer make, but thanks, and thanks'."

"Gloria, you have fashioned a home for all who are drawn to the inn and you are the most gracious hostess. I have so enjoyed my time here that I have no desire to find other accommodations."

He added, "You are all gifts to me, and you have all touched my life in myriad ways. Thank you."

The group was silent for a bit, absorbing all of the vulnerabilities that were displayed by each and every one.

Gloria broke the silence by asking David to carve the turkey.

After the feast, no one went their separate ways. The company was too great to abandon, the atmosphere joy-filled and convivial as board games were set out and coffee and pie were distributed.

Mario was glad that Scrabble was not among the games, as it was special to him and David.

Later on that evening, as the group dispersed, Gloria and David snuggled on the couch in her parlor. Wordlessly, each said a prayer of thanks for the burgeoning relationship of two people from divergent walks of life who miraculously found each other on their journey to a new life.

Mario was so grateful that the adoption process was nearing the end. He texted Debra one morning after he set his pot of sauce on the stove.

I have a favor to ask you. I need to get Joni's room ready for her homecoming, and I need a woman's touch to fill it with girly things. Can we go shopping on Monday?

Sure! What will be the motif?

I know that Joni likes unicorns most of all.

Great! I know just where to go.

Thank you, thank you, Debra! You are a lifesaver!!!!!

On Monday, the two set out for Linens and Discoveries in Mount Olive, about 15 minutes away and a larger metropolis than Oakview.

There were all kinds of unicorn offerings, and they chose a purple theme with curtains, bedspread, and pillows. Mario also ordered a twin bed, night stand, rocker and dresser. A giant stuffed purple unicorn would have a prominent place atop the rocker.

Debra asked Mario if Joni would be needing clothing, and he declared himself clueless. Just in case, they headed out to the nearest Kohl's and loaded up on size 11 clothes and outerwear. Mario knew that there was no way that she could have worn a larger size than 11, as petite as she was.

A few days after Thanksgiving, Cassie, David, Jenny Cooper and her parents traveled to Sacramento for the state contest for Poetry Comes Alive.

Each county in California had representation—a winner and a second-place contestant, in case the winner fell ill. For Bennington, second place fell to Carter Jones, who had prepared his two poems.

Jenny recited the Cummings poem, and "Caged Bird" by Maya Angelou. She came in third place, but did an excellent job. The competition was incredibly stiff. A student from Riverside STEAM Academy took first place and will move on to the national contest in Washington, D.C.

Cassie said her thanks to Jenny and her goodbyes to the Cooper and Jones families before turning to her father and hugging him.

"Dad, thank you so much for coming all this way with me. It meant the world to me."

"Cassie, I enjoyed it immensely! Well, since our Jenny isn't advancing, I hope that the winner does California proud in the national competition."

"Hey, our flight isn't until the morning. Why don't we do the town tonight and have dinner someplace fabulous!" Cassie suggested.

"Brilliant idea!!!" David replied.

They visited the state capitol and the Vietnam War Memorial in the northeast part of it, plus Old Sacramento, which covers eight blocks of historic buildings along the city's waterfront.

Margaritas in hand at La Terraza, they enjoyed the live music while nibbling on chips and guacamole.

Cassie decided to dip into her question box, which stood closed for so long.

"Tell me, Dad. Did you have a good relationship with Constance?"

"Oh, Cassie! I thought that we were soulmates, destined to be together forever. We loved the environment of Notre Dame and our shared love of literature. We lived together in this tiny apartment and lived on ramen. And we loved every moment of it."

He continued, "When we found out that Constance was pregnant, everything shifted. We were just finishing grad school and had plans—so many grandiose plans. We decided to give you up for adoption to a couple heading to California. And I understand that you had a great life with your adoptive parents."

"Yes, I did. They were the best. I had no desire to find you and Constance.   But I am glad that I did!"

"I am as well, my sweet. I am as well."

With that, David grabbed his daughter in a fierce hug, reaffirming all of the decisions he made to be near her.

With Christmas on the horizon, Mario took to the internet to do his shopping for the two most important women in his life.

From a company that personalizes just about everything, he found matching aprons that said *Daddy* and *Daddy's Sous Chef*. Those would be worn at home, not at the Boys and Girls Club.

He also personalized a chef's uniform for Debra, inscribed with *Chef Debra* and *Pizza Project #2*. He decided to wait to include her last name on the uniform.

The most important gift was purchased after Mario had a man-to-man talk with Bobby about giving his blessing upon his marriage to Debra, if she will have him.

"Cool! Really cool!" was Bobby's response, and Mario set out to the same jeweler where Buddy had purchased Sandy's ring.

On Christmas Eve, Mario signed the final adoption
papers and ventured over to the Collins home to fetch Joni.

He paused in his car outside of the home.

A daughter. He was going to have someone in his life
for whom he is responsible and who will change the
trajectory of his world.

When they returned to the Pizza Project, Mario and
Joni made the 10-step commute to their quarters. Mario was
anxious to show his new daughter her room.

"Oh, Mr. Mario! It's beautiful! Thank you so much!"

"Joni, you can call me Daddy from now on."

He hugged his China doll tightly, never wanting to let
her go.

Epilogue

Christmas Day settled briskly upon Oakview, bringing joy in myriad ways to its citizens as they enjoyed the festivities and gathered around tables laden with holiday treats.

For Laney and Scott, both sober now for many months, their shared recovery had wrought a peacefulness in both of them. What started out as a supportive friendship had bloomed into romance on their road to sobriety.

It turned out that Scott majored in journalism in college before entering the pizza business. After he penned a four-part series on his recovery journey for the paper, Laney hired him at the *Register* to write human interest stories. And, thankfully, he was a citizen of good standing in Oakview once more.

Mayor Max and Harley were relishing their role as parents to little EJ, a busy 19-month-old who seemed to have skipped walking and went right to running—everywhere. Inspired by Mario, and with their own successful adoption story in mind, they decided to adopt a little girl. That would make their family complete, said Max as they met with an adoption agent. A complete, blessed family.

Bobby and Maritza and Porter and Sophia were all still going strong, enjoying double dates and watching Bobby play Lions football on Friday nights. With collegiate commitments on the horizon, Sophia applied to several colleges utilizing the early-decision option. She was accepted to many of them, including the University of San Diego, her top choice. She and Porter would be experiencing the collegiate lifestyle together as Toreros.

Cassie and Pete gave her father the best Christmas gift of all. He was going to be a grandfather!

Uncharacteristically, David shed tears of joy when they gave him the news, gifting him a shirt that declared "World's Best Grandpa." Constance was slated to return the first of the year, so she would have much happy news to come home to, along with her T-shirt emblazoned "World's Best Grandma."

The brand-spanking-new Sandy's Dandies was slated to open the first Saturday in January. Buddy was proud of his wife's success, and offered to come work with her, but she declined. Buddy was established at the Pizza Project, and Mario needed him more than ever as his hours were being shortened in his quest to become a good father.

Maisie was accustomed to dining solo on holidays, as her husband had passed away five years earlier and the couple was childless. That sad fact became a memory when seated at her Christmas table were Bill and his new girlfriend Veronica. The two met at Oakview First Bank and had been inseparable since.

Gloria and David were planning for their first vacation together as a couple. They would be visiting San Francisco during David's semester break and were eagerly anticipating some precious time away.

An internet search netted Gloria's discovery of a few maid agencies that offer temporary live-in services, and she jumped at the chance to hire a team. Thankfully, there were no new guests slated to arrive during their rendezvous.

Steve and Emi tied the knot on December 15, and Mario was proud to have Debra on his arm, his precious plus one. In April, the Bridges clan would announce the impending birth of their son, much to the delight of Jacob and Beth.

With Bobby and Joni taking advantage of the arcade in PP #1, Mario took Debra's hand and walked her across the street to the gazebo precisely at 10:00 Christmas morning. Buddy and Sandy were surreptitiously hiding in Maisie's alcove, ready to record video of the proposal and hugging in the chilly Christmas air.

The Bertollis and the Wilsons would become a blended family, and would soon need a larger home for their brood. Bobby had already taken to Joni, who would be the sibling he never had. He loved to give her piggyback rides and delighted in her sweet laughter. He even participated in tea parties in what he called her "unicorn room."

And in June, with mostly everyone in Oakview as witness to their nuptials in the town square, Constance would declare Mario and Debra husband and wife.

And Mario's Karaoke Angel would be his forever.

About the Author

When Tanya Katnic was reading a romance novel every week, her husband Andrew challenged her to write a book of her own. She made a promise to herself that one day she would pen her own novel. Fast-forward past her career as a high school English and journalism teacher, and the promise was fulfilled. *A Recipe For Love* is her sophomore tome, an engaging sequel to *Our Mother Away From Home.*